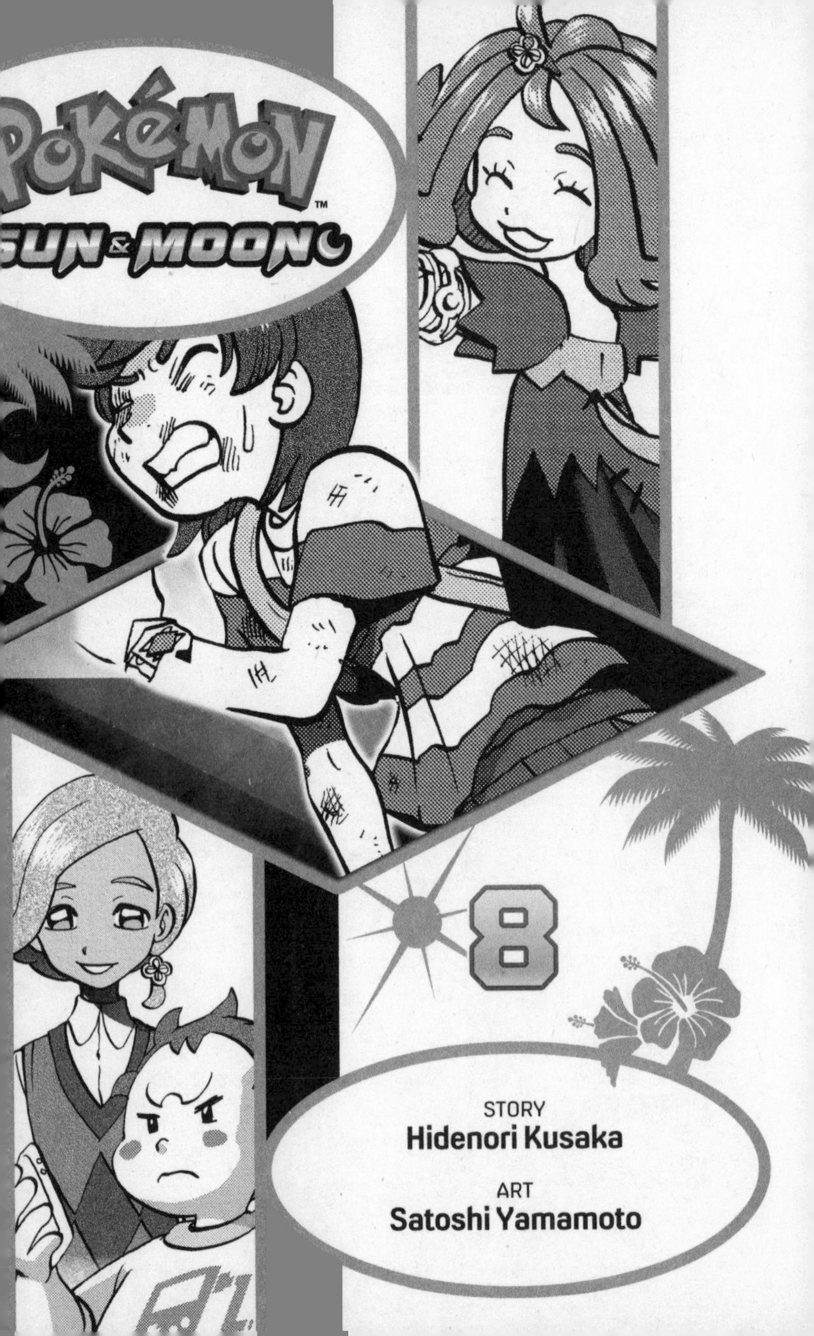

Pokémon™ Sun & Moon

8

STORY
Hidenori Kusaka

ART
Satoshi Yamamoto

Introduction

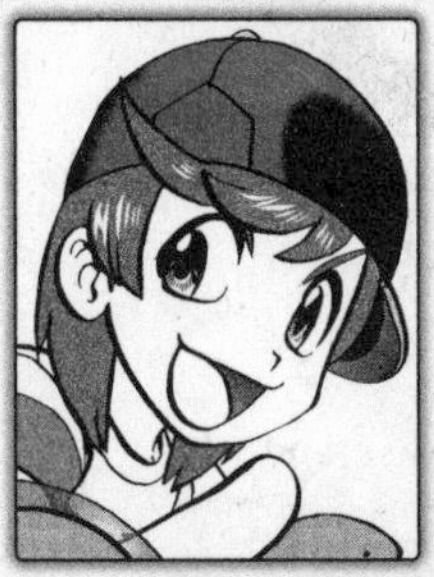

Sun

One of the main characters of this tale. A young Pokémon Trainer who makes a living doing all sorts of odd jobs, including working as a delivery boy. His dream is to save up a million dollars!

Moon

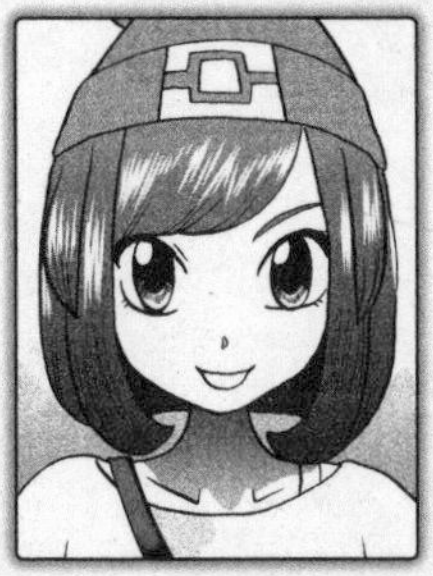

Another of the main characters of this tale. A pharmacist who has traveled to Alola from a faraway region. She is a self-confident, original thinker. She is also an excellent archer.

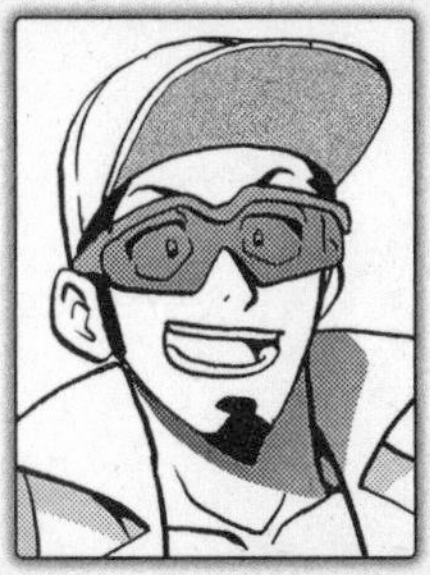

Professor Kukui

A Pokémon researcher with a laboratory on Melemele Island. An expert on Pokémon moves who likes to experience these Pokémon moves used against himself!

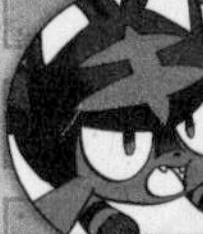

Dollar (Torracat)

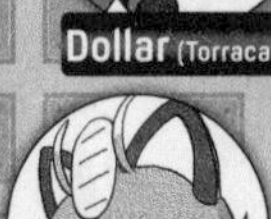

Cent (Alolan Meowth)

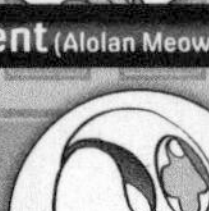

Quarter (Wishiwashi)

Kiawe, Mallow, Lana

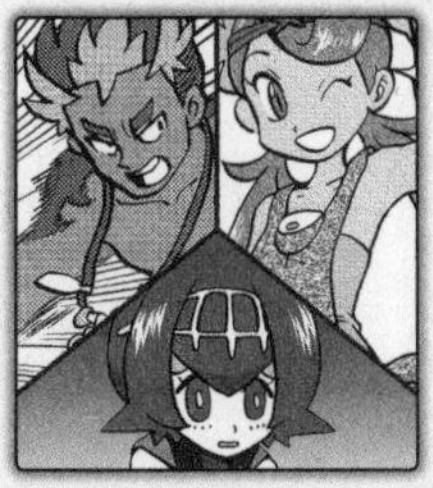

Skilled Trainers and the trial captains of Akala Island.

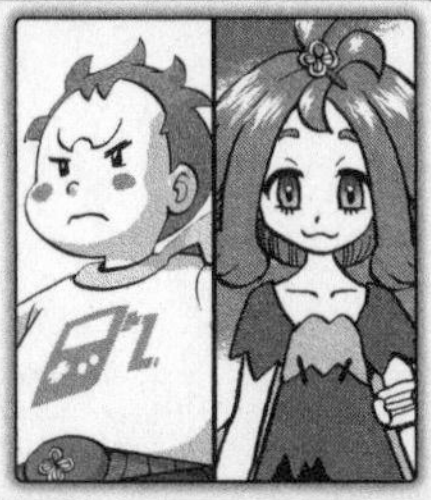

Acerola/ Sophocles

Skilled Trainers and the trial captains of Ula'ula Island.

Character

Guzma

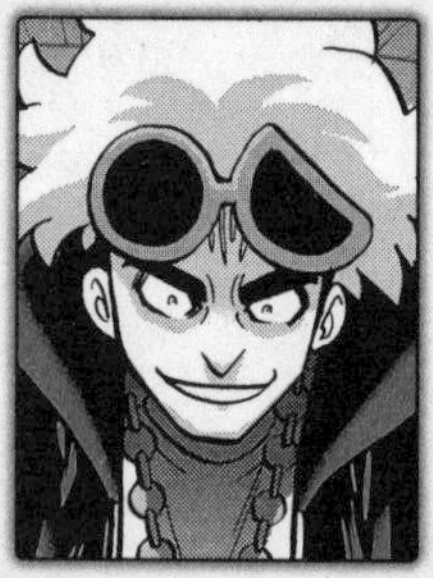

The leader of Team Skull, an evil organization that is causing trouble all over the Alolan region.

Lillie

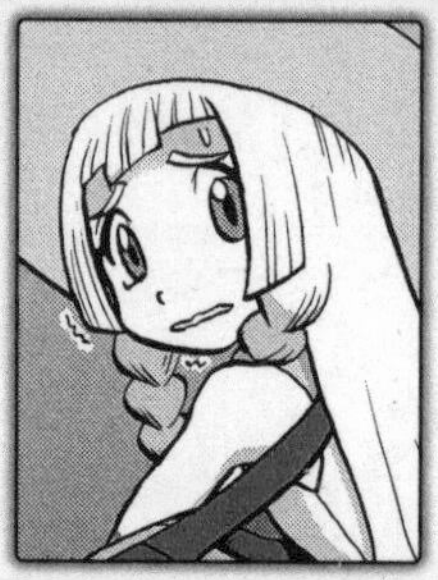

A timid girl found washed up on the beach. She carries a strange Pokémon whom she calls Nebby.

Gladion

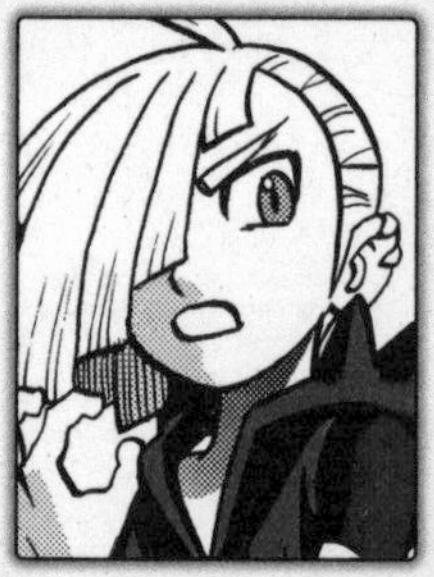

A loner with a mysterious Pokémon named Type: Null. Why is he so interested in a mysterious rift in the sky...?

The Story Thus Far...

Moon and Sun meet in the Alola region, a flower-filled vacation paradise. There's trouble in paradise though, because the guardians of the Alolan Islands, called Tapu, are agitated. Sun is chosen to soothe the Tapu's anger, and Moon decides to assist him. On their journey, they meet a mysterious girl named Lillie whose Pokémon Nebby, a Cosmog, creates rifts in the sky. Ultra Beasts are arriving through these portals from an alternate dimension, and one of them drags Guzma, the boss of nefarious Team Skull, to the other side. As fierce battles with Ultra Beasts rage throughout the islands, two International Police officers arrive on the scene and ask Sun and Moon for help. Sun agrees in exchange for...what else? Money. While Moon and Officer Anabel head to Poni Island to repel attacking Ultra Beasts, Sun goes to deliver a special Berry to calm Tapu Fini while collecting Zygarde cells for the police along the way. When the berry is stolen by a gang of Crabrawler led by a powerful Crabominable, newly appointed Kahuna Hapu helps Sun retrieve it. But how will our friends stop the Ultra Beasts once and for all...?

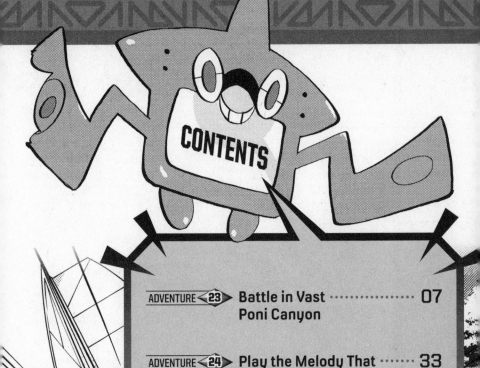

CONTENTS

Zzt zzt... ♫

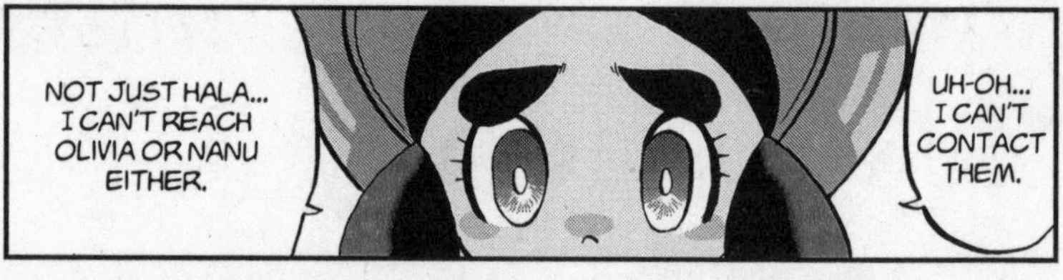
UH-OH... I CAN'T CONTACT THEM.
NOT JUST HALA... I CAN'T REACH OLIVIA OR NANU EITHER.

Adventure 23 Battle in Vast Poni Canyon

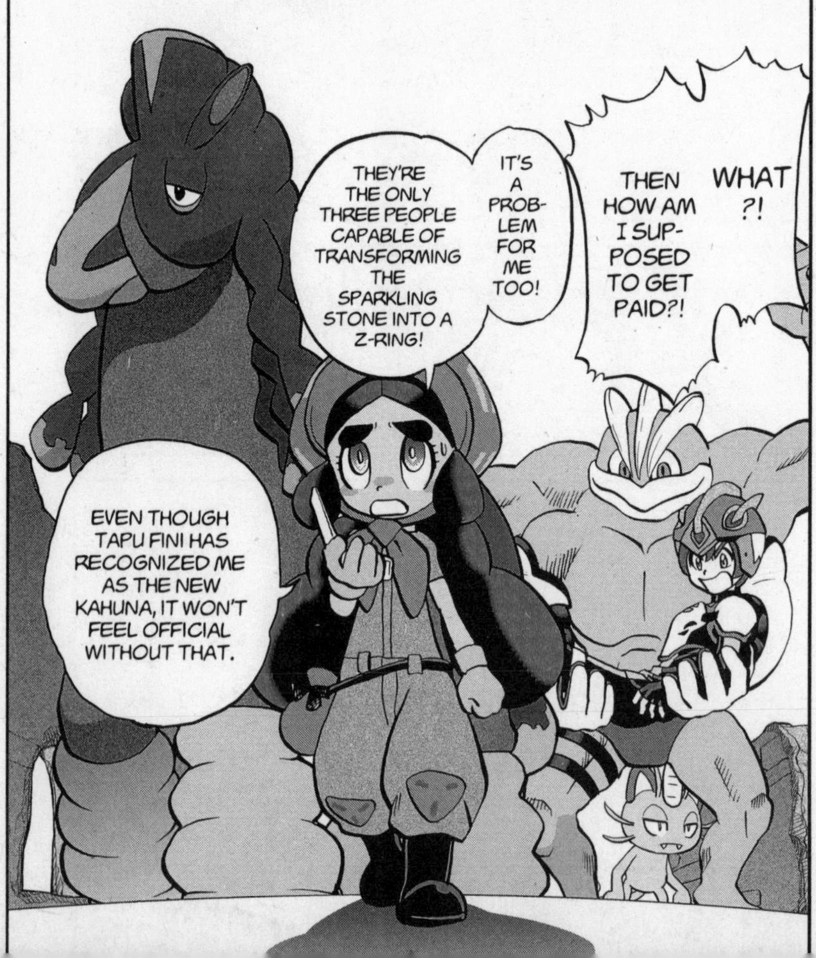
WHAT?!
THEN HOW AM I SUP-POSED TO GET PAID?!
IT'S A PROB-LEM FOR ME TOO!
THEY'RE THE ONLY THREE PEOPLE CAPABLE OF TRANSFORMING THE SPARKLING STONE INTO A Z-RING!
EVEN THOUGH TAPU FINI HAS RECOGNIZED ME AS THE NEW KAHUNA, IT WON'T FEEL OFFICIAL WITHOUT THAT.

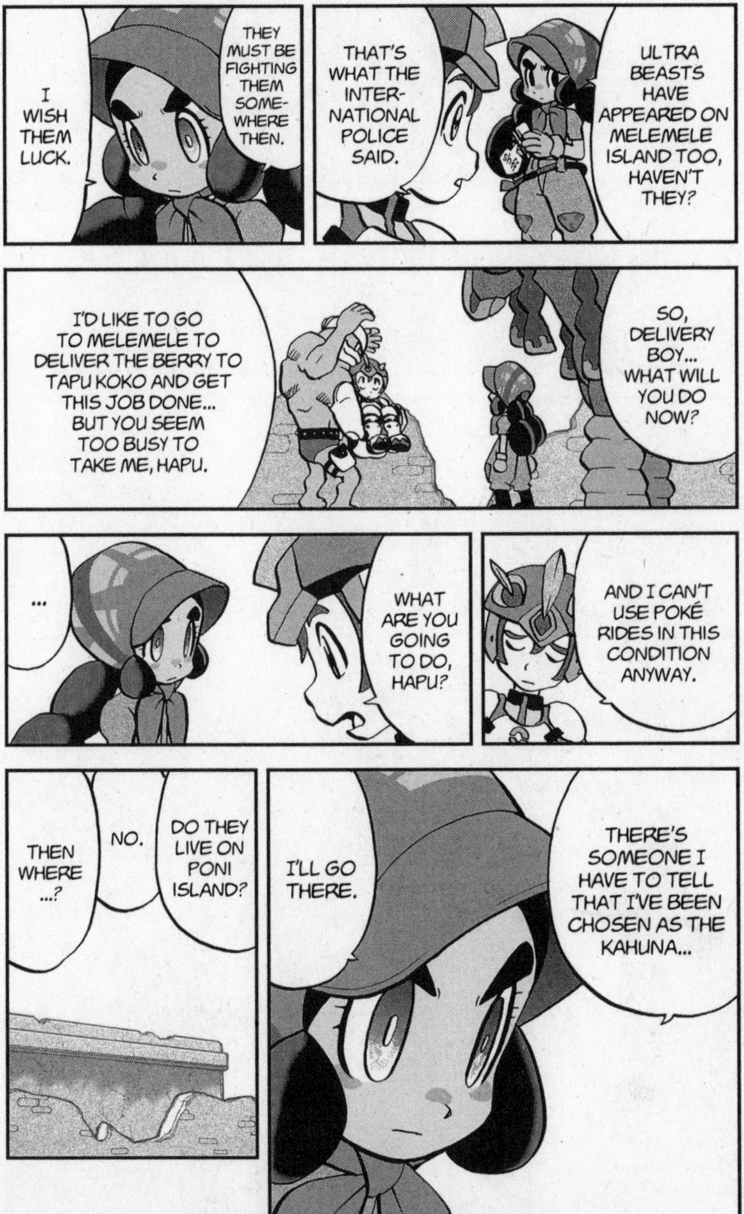
ULTRA BEASTS HAVE APPEARED ON MELEMELE ISLAND TOO, HAVEN'T THEY?
shff
THAT'S WHAT THE INTER-NATIONAL POLICE SAID.
THEY MUST BE FIGHTING THEM SOME-WHERE THEN.
I WISH THEM LUCK.
SO, DELIVERY BOY... WHAT WILL YOU DO NOW?
I'D LIKE TO GO TO MELEMELE TO DELIVER THE BERRY TO TAPU KOKO AND GET THIS JOB DONE... BUT YOU SEEM TOO BUSY TO TAKE ME, HAPU.
AND I CAN'T USE POKÉ RIDES IN THIS CONDITION ANYWAY.
WHAT ARE YOU GOING TO DO, HAPU?
...
THERE'S SOMEONE I HAVE TO TELL THAT I'VE BEEN CHOSEN AS THE KAHUNA...
I'LL GO THERE.
DO THEY LIVE ON PONI ISLAND?
NO.
THEN WHERE ...?

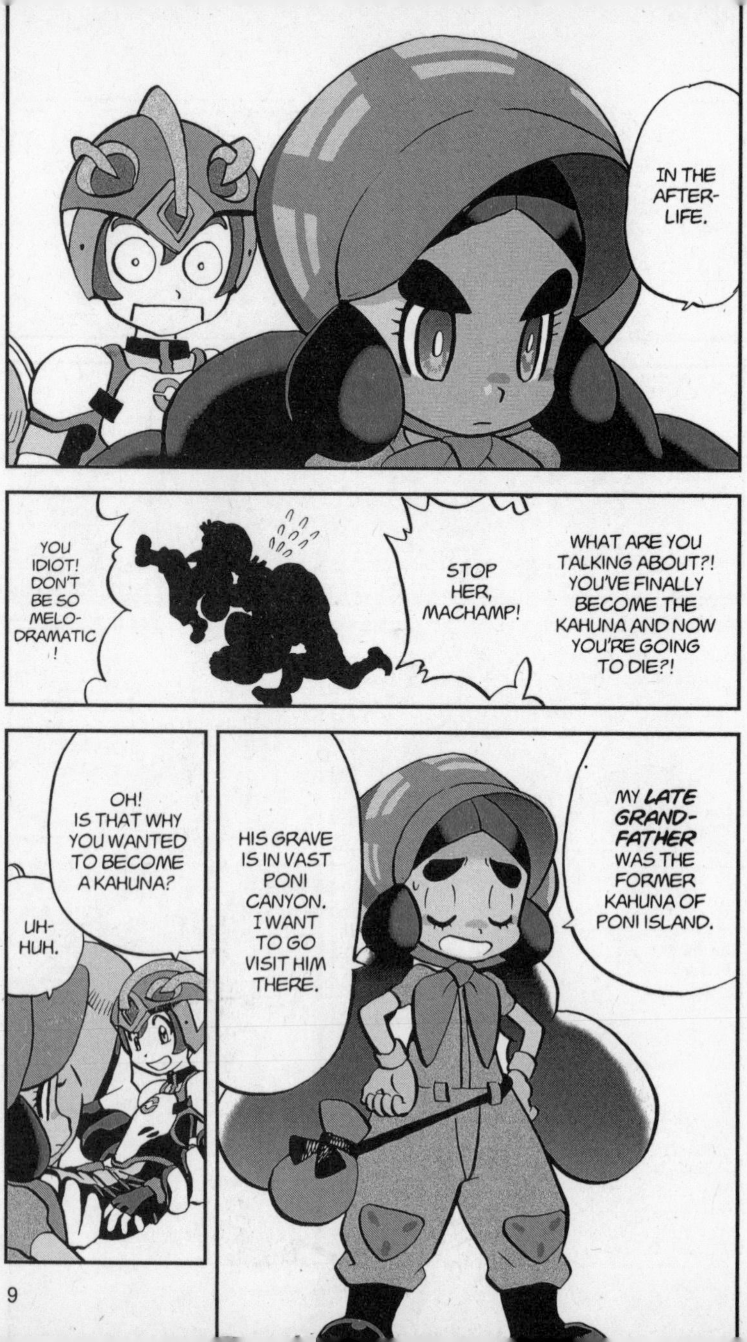
IN THE AFTER-LIFE.
WHAT ARE YOU TALKING ABOUT?! YOU'VE FINALLY BECOME THE KAHUNA AND NOW YOU'RE GOING TO DIE?!
STOP HER, MACHAMP!
YOU IDIOT! DON'T BE SO MELO-DRAMATIC!
MY **LATE GRAND-FATHER** WAS THE FORMER KAHUNA OF PONI ISLAND.
HIS GRAVE IS IN VAST PONI CANYON. I WANT TO GO VISIT HIM THERE.
OH! IS THAT WHY YOU WANTED TO BECOME A KAHUNA?
UH-HUH.

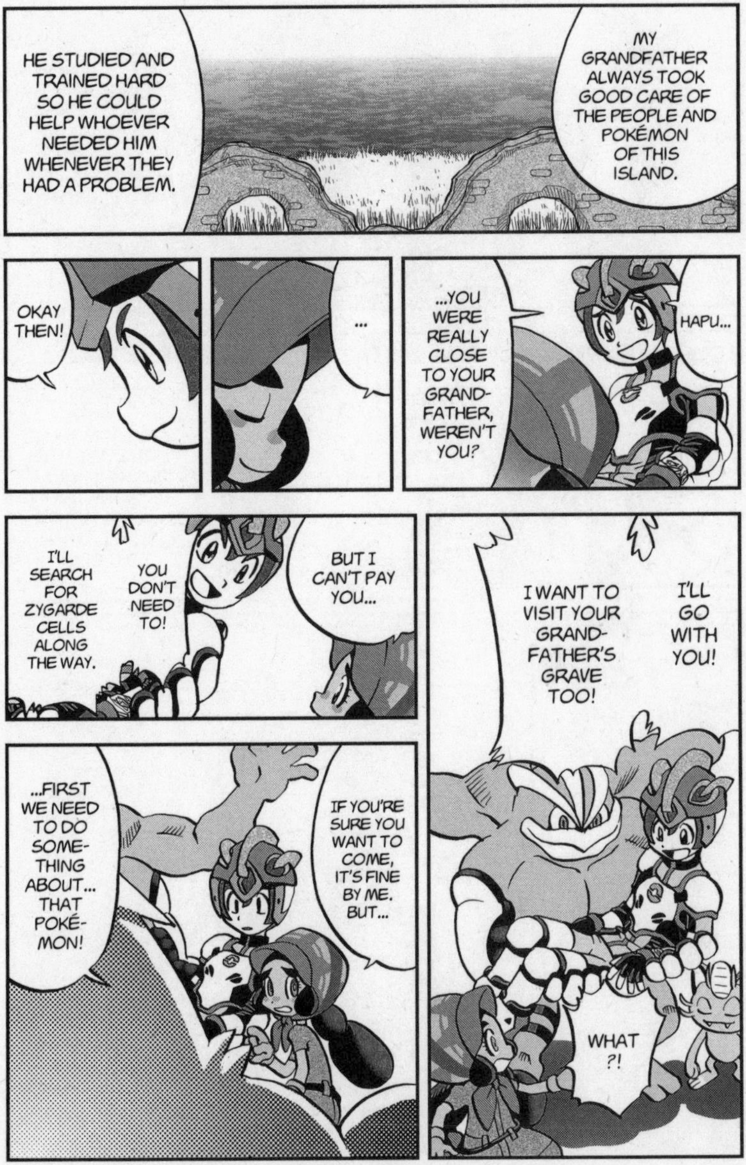
MY GRANDFATHER ALWAYS TOOK GOOD CARE OF THE PEOPLE AND POKéMON OF THIS ISLAND.
HE STUDIED AND TRAINED HARD SO HE COULD HELP WHOEVER NEEDED HIM WHENEVER THEY HAD A PROBLEM.
HAPU...
...YOU WERE REALLY CLOSE TO YOUR GRAND-FATHER, WEREN'T YOU?
...
OKAY THEN!
I'LL GO WITH YOU!
I WANT TO VISIT YOUR GRAND-FATHER'S GRAVE TOO!
WHAT ?!
BUT I CAN'T PAY YOU...
YOU DON'T NEED TO!
I'LL SEARCH FOR ZYGARDE CELLS ALONG THE WAY.
IF YOU'RE SURE YOU WANT TO COME, IT'S FINE BY ME. BUT...
...FIRST WE NEED TO DO SOME-THING ABOUT... THAT POKÉ-MON!

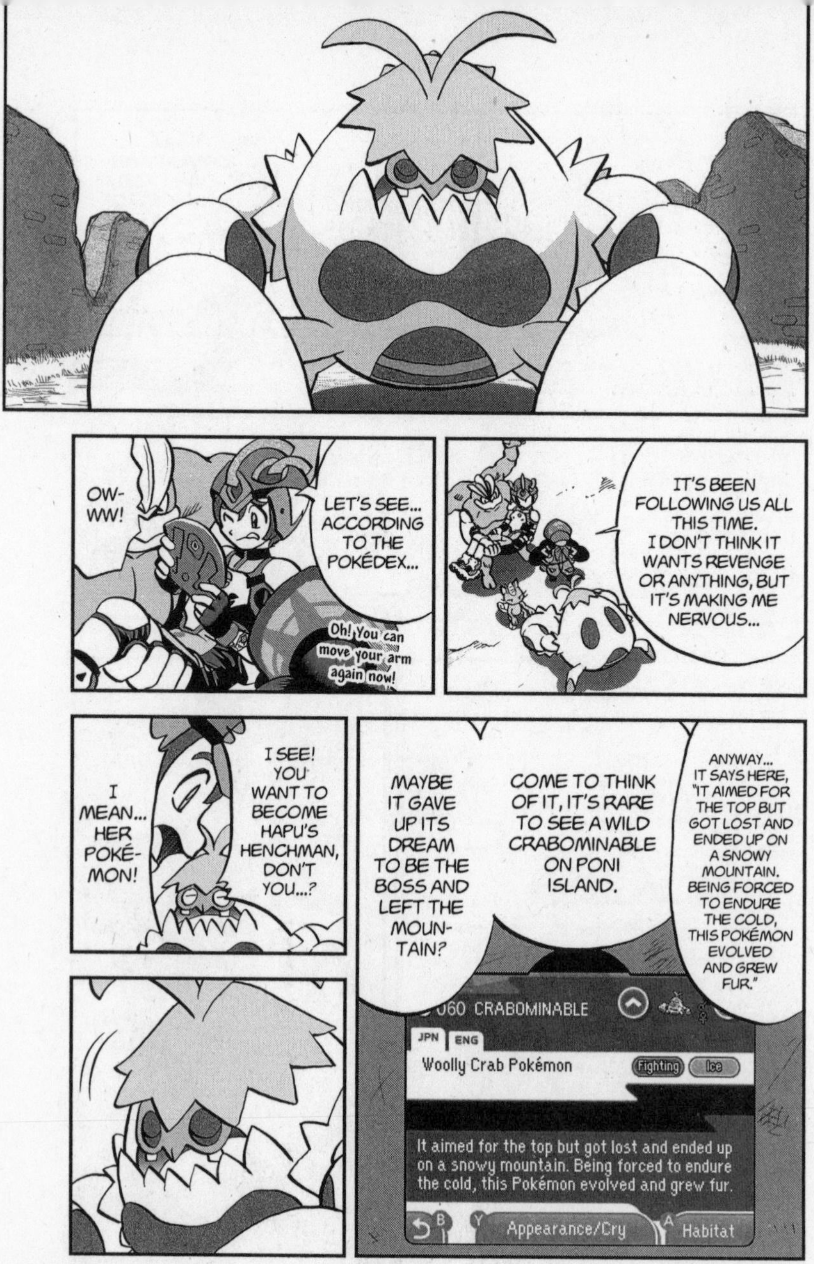
IT'S BEEN FOLLOWING US ALL THIS TIME. I DON'T THINK IT WANTS REVENGE OR ANYTHING, BUT IT'S MAKING ME NERVOUS...
LET'S SEE... ACCORDING TO THE POKÉDEX...
OW-WW!
Oh! You can move your arm again now!
ANYWAY... IT SAYS HERE, "IT AIMED FOR THE TOP BUT GOT LOST AND ENDED UP ON A SNOWY MOUNTAIN. BEING FORCED TO ENDURE THE COLD, THIS POKÉMON EVOLVED AND GREW FUR."
COME TO THINK OF IT, IT'S RARE TO SEE A WILD CRABOMINABLE ON PONI ISLAND.
MAYBE IT GAVE UP ITS DREAM TO BE THE BOSS AND LEFT THE MOUN-TAIN?
060 CRABOMINABLE
JPN
ENG
Woolly Crab Pokémon
Fighting
Ice
It aimed for the top but got lost and ended up on a snowy mountain. Being forced to endure the cold, this Pokémon evolved and grew fur.
Appearance/Cry
Habitat
I SEE! YOU WANT TO BECOME HAPU'S HENCHMAN, DON'T YOU...?
I MEAN... HER POKÉ-MON!

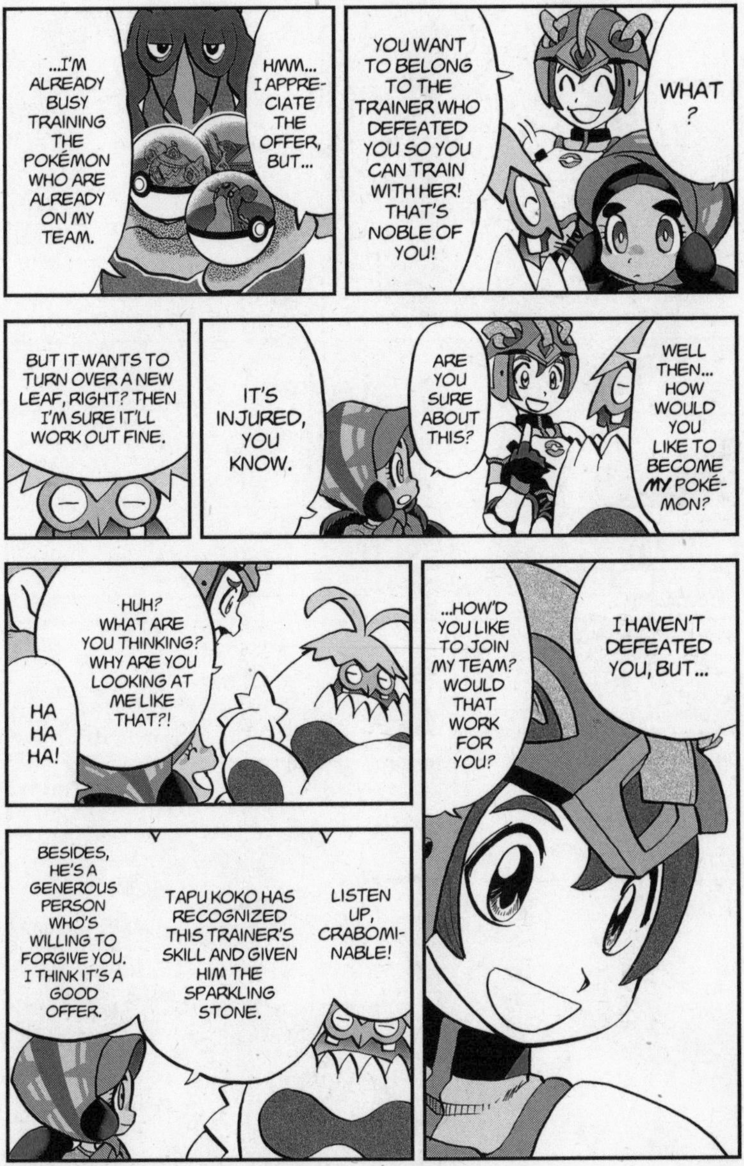
WHAT?
YOU WANT TO BELONG TO THE TRAINER WHO DEFEATED YOU SO YOU CAN TRAIN WITH HER! THAT'S NOBLE OF YOU!
HMM... I APPRECIATE THE OFFER, BUT...
...I'M ALREADY BUSY TRAINING THE POKÉMON WHO ARE ALREADY ON MY TEAM.
WELL THEN... HOW WOULD YOU LIKE TO BECOME MY POKÉMON?
ARE YOU SURE ABOUT THIS?
IT'S INJURED, YOU KNOW.
BUT IT WANTS TO TURN OVER A NEW LEAF, RIGHT? THEN I'M SURE IT'LL WORK OUT FINE.
I HAVEN'T DEFEATED YOU, BUT...
...HOW'D YOU LIKE TO JOIN MY TEAM? WOULD THAT WORK FOR YOU?
HUH? WHAT ARE YOU THINKING? WHY ARE YOU LOOKING AT ME LIKE THAT?!
HA HA HA!
LISTEN UP, CRABOMINABLE!
TAPU KOKO HAS RECOGNIZED THIS TRAINER'S SKILL AND GIVEN HIM THE SPARKLING STONE.
BESIDES, HE'S A GENEROUS PERSON WHO'S WILLING TO FORGIVE YOU. I THINK IT'S A GOOD OFFER.

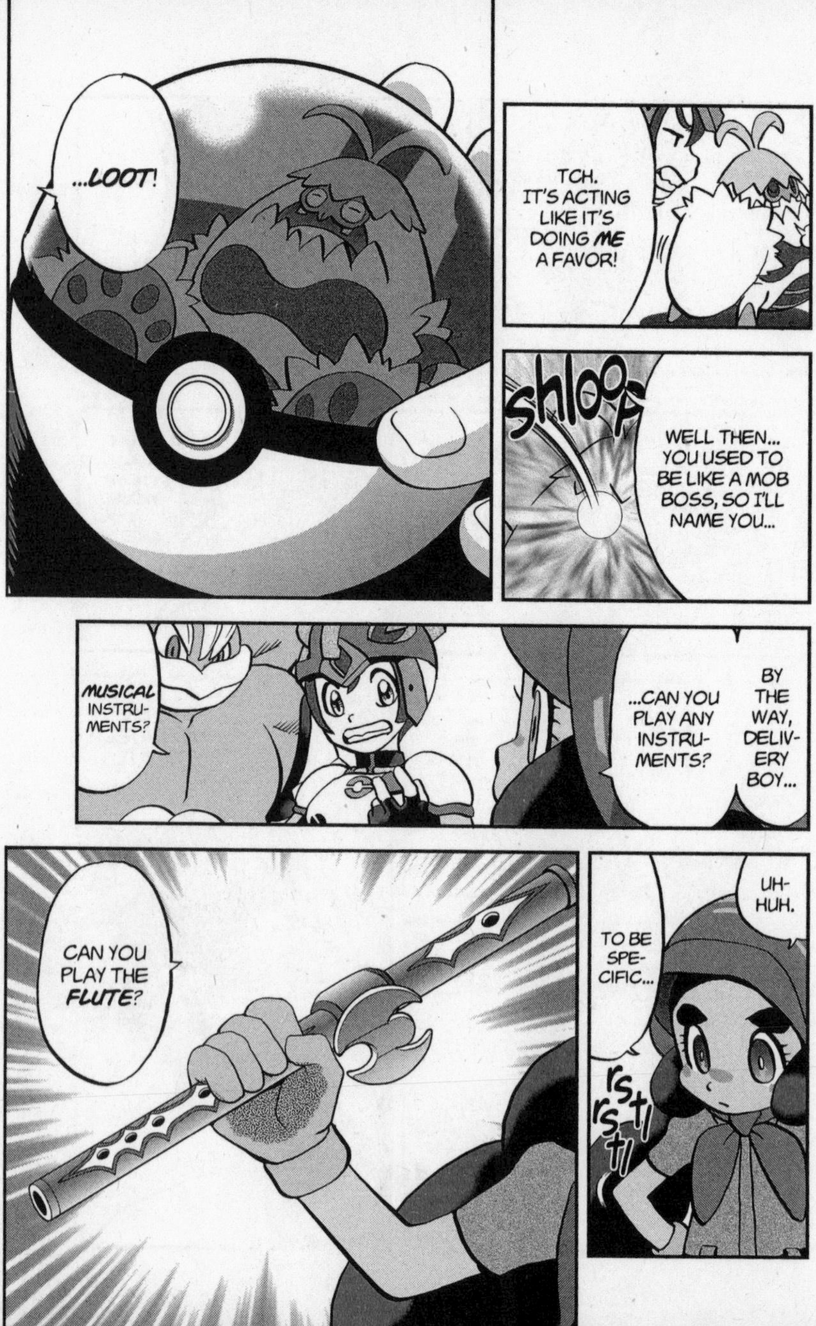
TCH. IT'S ACTING LIKE IT'S DOING ME A FAVOR!
shloop
WELL THEN... YOU USED TO BE LIKE A MOB BOSS, SO I'LL NAME YOU...
...LOOT!
BY THE WAY, DELIVERY BOY...
...CAN YOU PLAY ANY INSTRUMENTS?
MUSICAL INSTRUMENTS?
UH-HUH.
TO BE SPECIFIC...
rstl rstl
CAN YOU PLAY THE FLUTE?

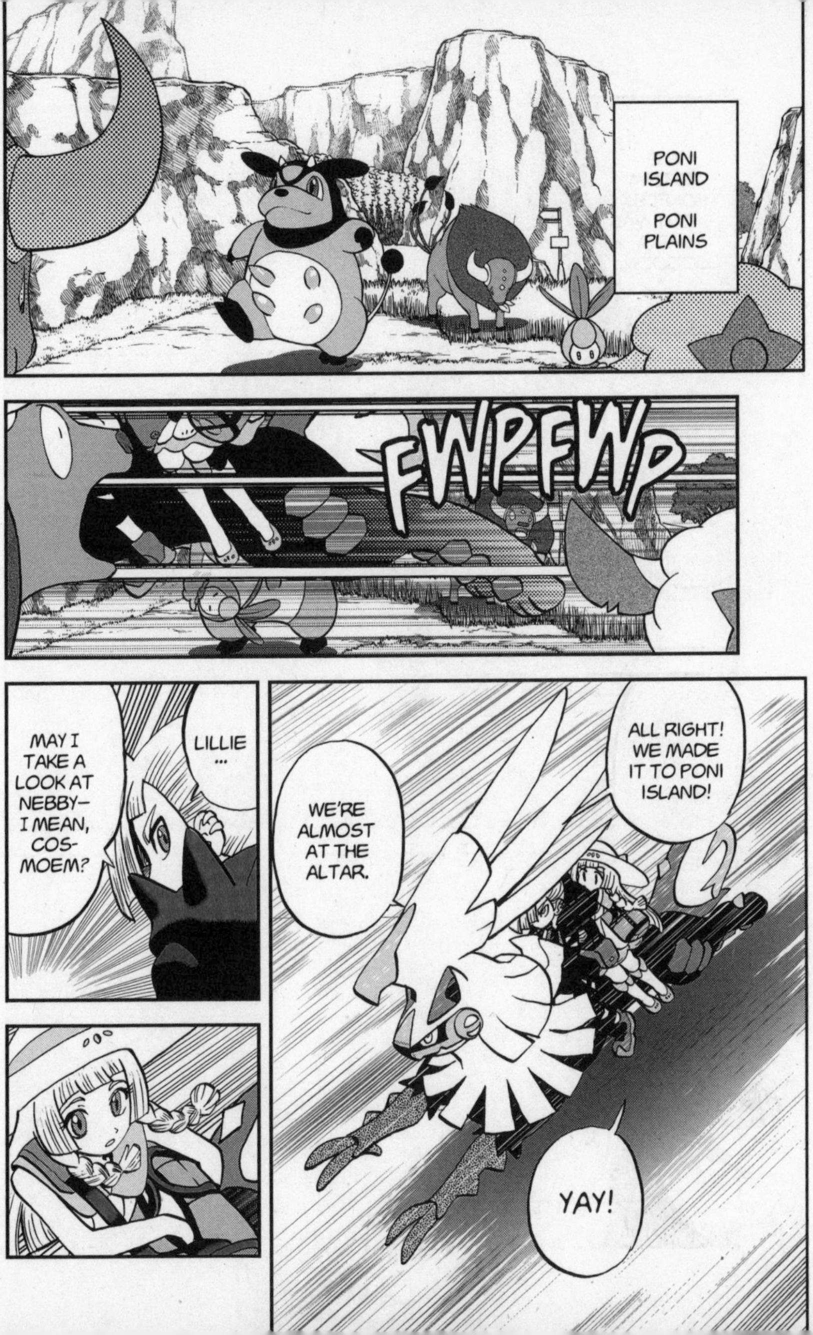
PONI ISLAND
PONI PLAINS
FWPFWP
ALL RIGHT! WE MADE IT TO PONI ISLAND!
WE'RE ALMOST AT THE ALTAR.
YAY!
LILLIE ...
MAY I TAKE A LOOK AT NEBBY—I MEAN, COS-MOEM?

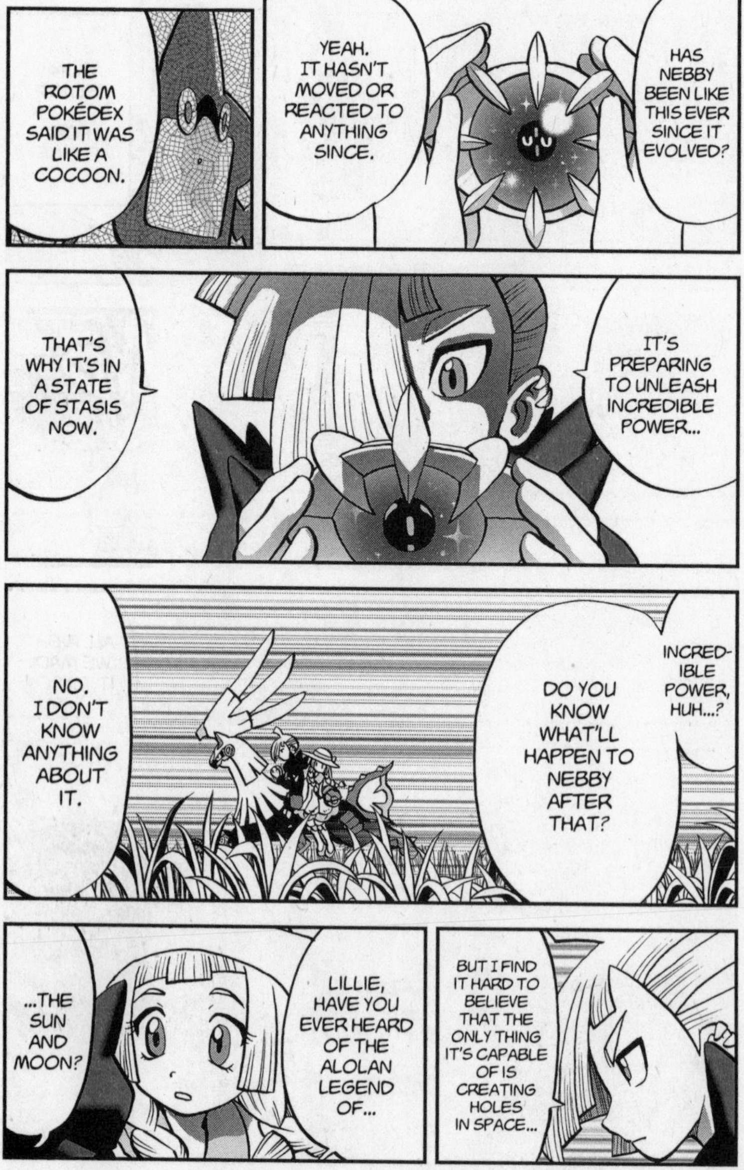
HAS NEBBY BEEN LIKE THIS EVER SINCE IT EVOLVED?
YEAH. IT HASN'T MOVED OR REACTED TO ANYTHING SINCE.
THE ROTOM POKÉDEX SAID IT WAS LIKE A COCOON.
IT'S PREPARING TO UNLEASH INCREDIBLE POWER...
THAT'S WHY IT'S IN A STATE OF STASIS NOW.
INCRED-IBLE POWER, HUH...?
DO YOU KNOW WHAT'LL HAPPEN TO NEBBY AFTER THAT?
NO. I DON'T KNOW ANYTHING ABOUT IT.
BUT I FIND IT HARD TO BELIEVE THAT THE ONLY THING IT'S CAPABLE OF IS CREATING HOLES IN SPACE...
LILLIE, HAVE YOU EVER HEARD OF THE ALOLAN LEGEND OF...
...THE SUN AND MOON?

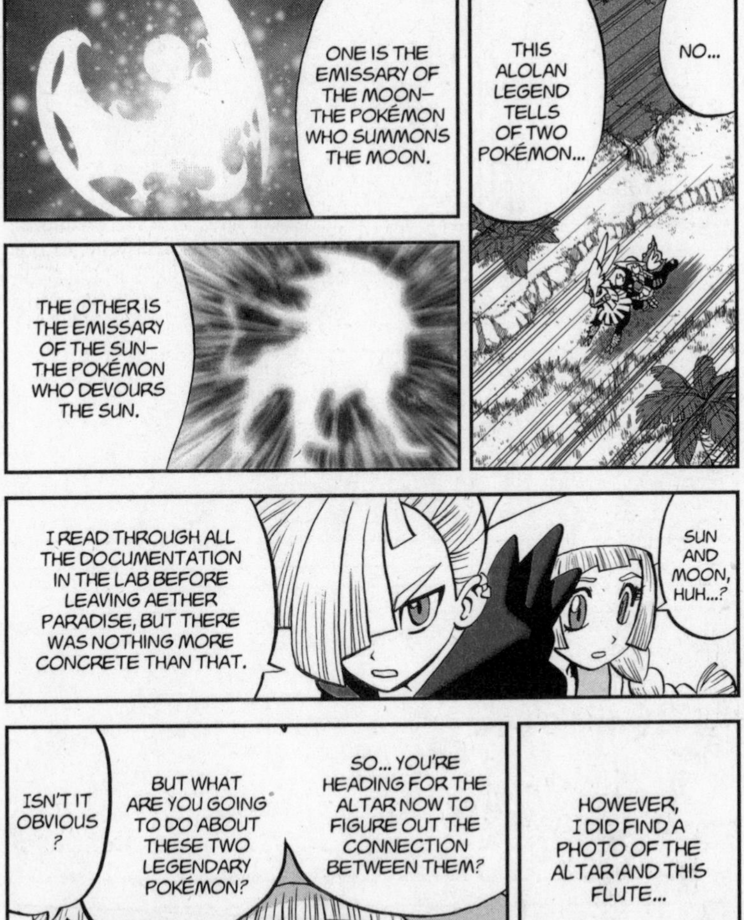
NO...
THIS ALOLAN LEGEND TELLS OF TWO POKÉMON...
ONE IS THE EMISSARY OF THE MOON— THE POKÉMON WHO SUMMONS THE MOON.
THE OTHER IS THE EMISSARY OF THE SUN— THE POKÉMON WHO DEVOURS THE SUN.
SUN AND MOON, HUH...?
I READ THROUGH ALL THE DOCUMENTATION IN THE LAB BEFORE LEAVING AETHER PARADISE, BUT THERE WAS NOTHING MORE CONCRETE THAN THAT.
HOWEVER, I DID FIND A PHOTO OF THE ALTAR AND THIS FLUTE...
SO... YOU'RE HEADING FOR THE ALTAR NOW TO FIGURE OUT THE CONNECTION BETWEEN THEM?
BUT WHAT ARE YOU GOING TO DO ABOUT THESE TWO LEGENDARY POKÉMON?
ISN'T IT OBVIOUS?

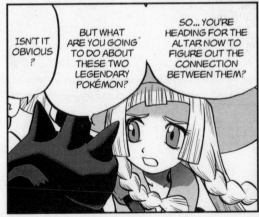

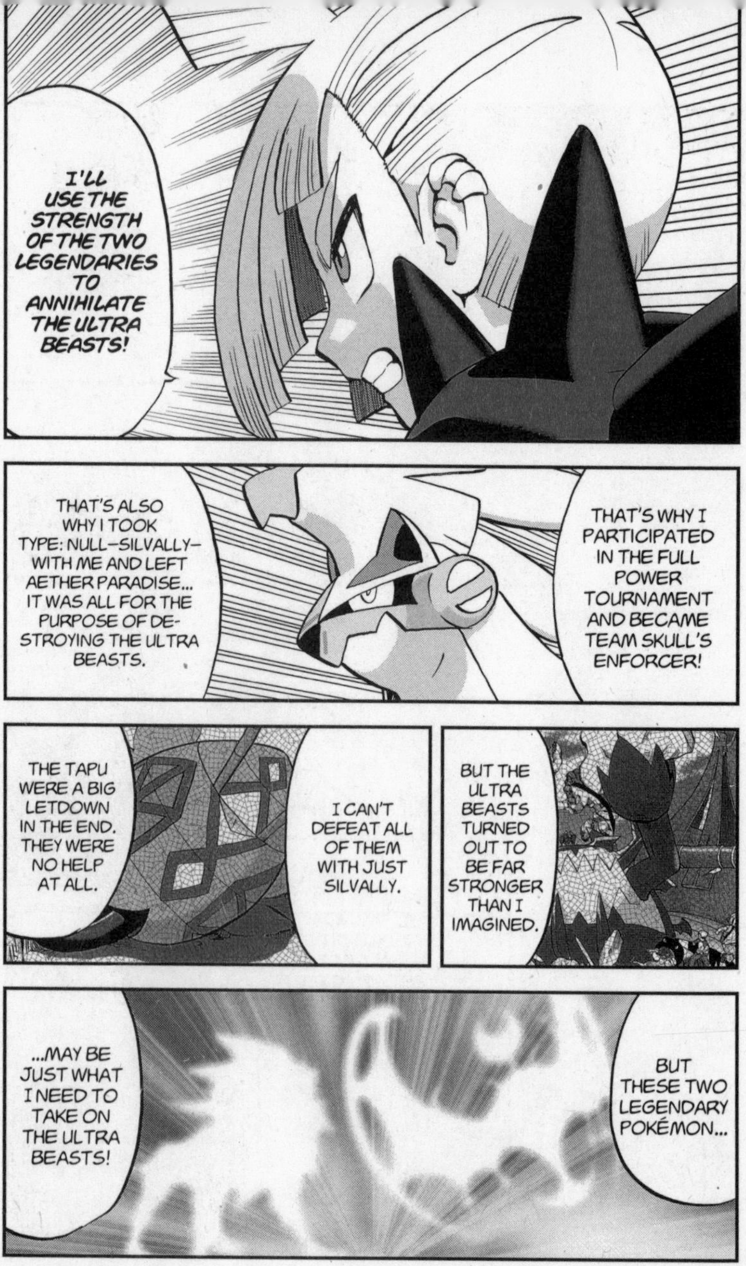
I'LL USE THE STRENGTH OF THE TWO LEGENDARIES TO ANNIHILATE THE ULTRA BEASTS!
THAT'S WHY I PARTICIPATED IN THE FULL POWER TOURNAMENT AND BECAME TEAM SKULL'S ENFORCER!
THAT'S ALSO WHY I TOOK TYPE: NULL—SILVALLY—WITH ME AND LEFT AETHER PARADISE... IT WAS ALL FOR THE PURPOSE OF DE-STROYING THE ULTRA BEASTS.
BUT THE ULTRA BEASTS TURNED OUT TO BE FAR STRONGER THAN I IMAGINED.
I CAN'T DEFEAT ALL OF THEM WITH JUST SILVALLY.
THE TAPU WERE A BIG LETDOWN IN THE END. THEY WERE NO HELP AT ALL.
BUT THESE TWO LEGENDARY POKÉMON...
...MAY BE JUST WHAT I NEED TO TAKE ON THE ULTRA BEASTS!

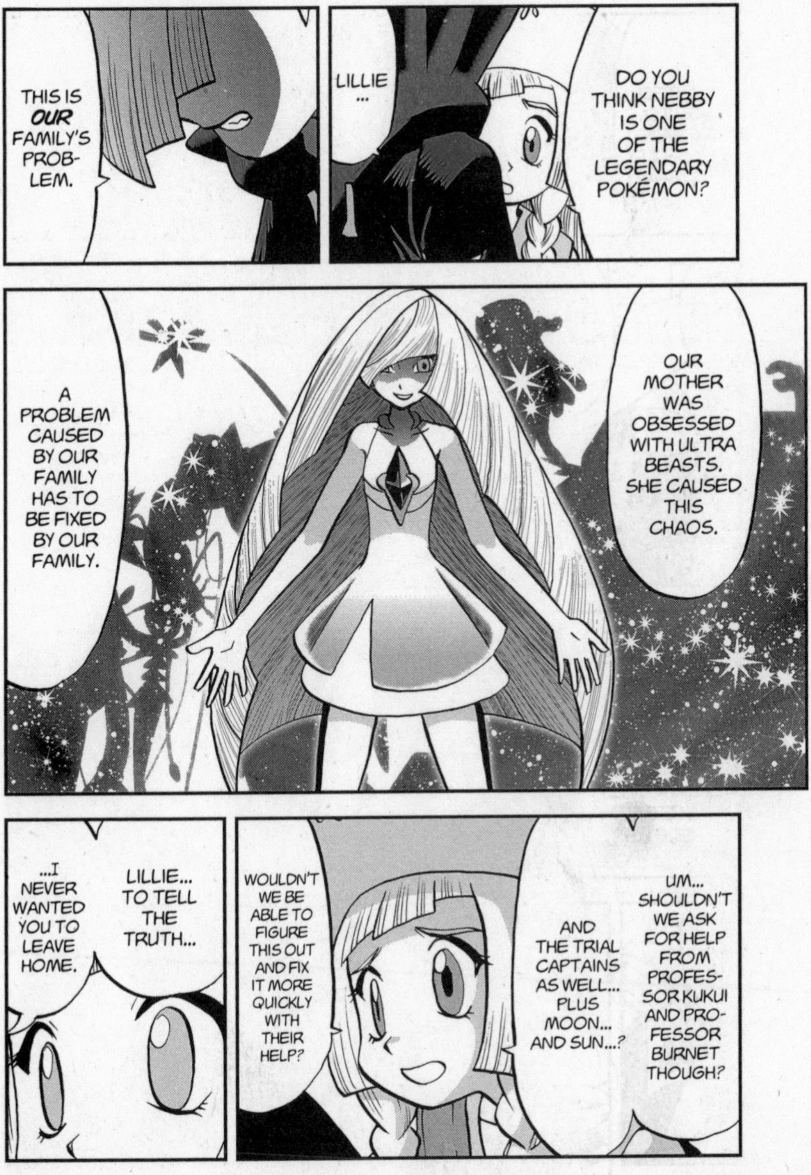
DO YOU THINK NEBBY IS ONE OF THE LEGENDARY POKÉMON?
LILLIE ...
THIS IS ***OUR*** FAMILY'S PROB-LEM.
OUR MOTHER WAS OBSESSED WITH ULTRA BEASTS. SHE CAUSED THIS CHAOS.
A PROBLEM CAUSED BY OUR FAMILY HAS TO BE FIXED BY OUR FAMILY.
UM... SHOULDN'T WE ASK FOR HELP FROM PROFES-SOR KUKUI AND PRO-FESSOR BURNET THOUGH?
AND THE TRIAL CAPTAINS AS WELL... PLUS MOON... AND SUN...?
WOULDN'T WE BE ABLE TO FIGURE THIS OUT AND FIX IT MORE QUICKLY WITH THEIR HELP?
LILLIE... TO TELL THE TRUTH...
...I NEVER WANTED YOU TO LEAVE HOME.

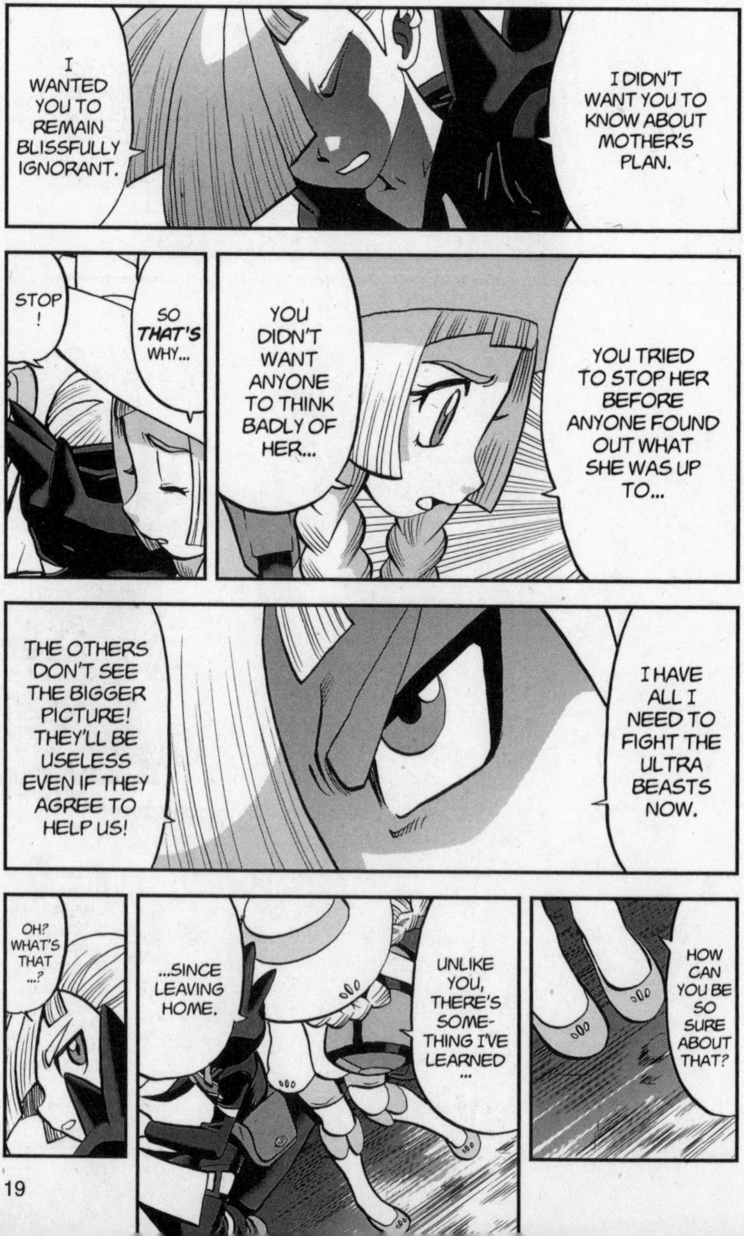
I DIDN'T WANT YOU TO KNOW ABOUT MOTHER'S PLAN.
I WANTED YOU TO REMAIN BLISSFULLY IGNORANT.
YOU TRIED TO STOP HER BEFORE ANYONE FOUND OUT WHAT SHE WAS UP TO...
YOU DIDN'T WANT ANYONE TO THINK BADLY OF HER...
SO *THAT'S* WHY...
STOP!
I HAVE ALL I NEED TO FIGHT THE ULTRA BEASTS NOW.
THE OTHERS DON'T SEE THE BIGGER PICTURE! THEY'LL BE USELESS EVEN IF THEY AGREE TO HELP US!
HOW CAN YOU BE SO SURE ABOUT THAT?
UNLIKE YOU, THERE'S SOMETHING I'VE LEARNED...
...SINCE LEAVING HOME.
OH? WHAT'S THAT...?

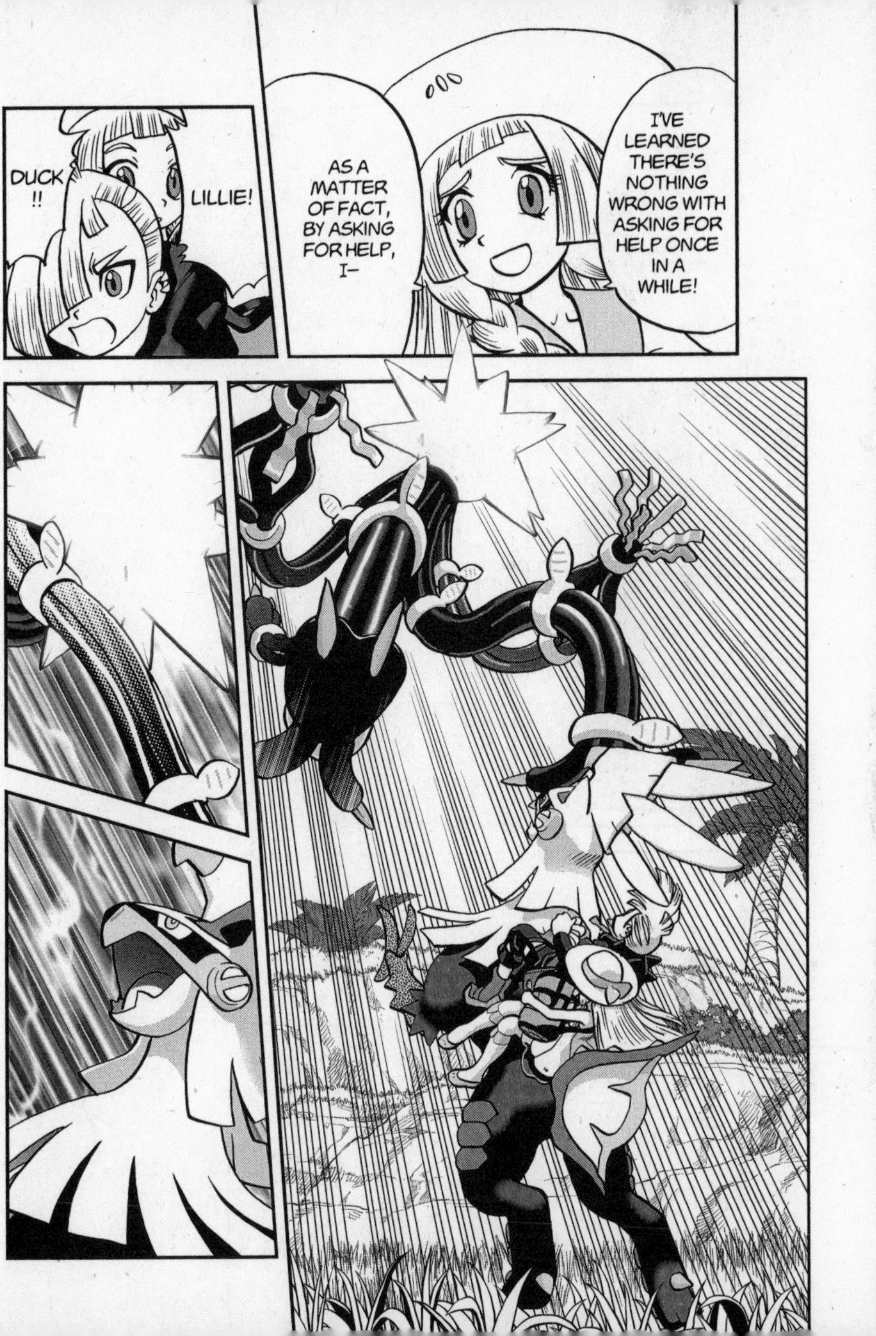
I'VE LEARNED THERE'S NOTHING WRONG WITH ASKING FOR HELP ONCE IN A WHILE!
AS A MATTER OF FACT, BY ASKING FOR HELP, I—
LILLIE!
DUCK !!

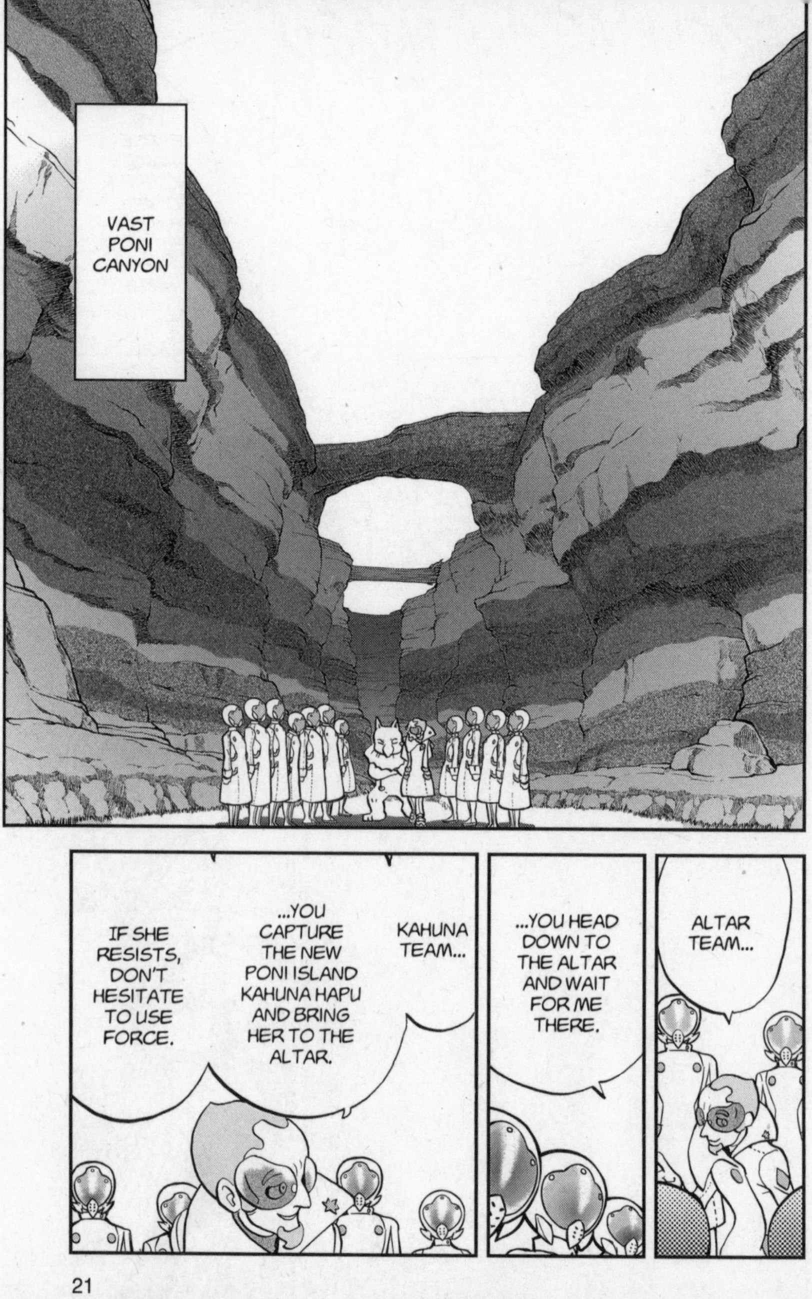
VAST PONI CANYON
ALTAR TEAM...
...YOU HEAD DOWN TO THE ALTAR AND WAIT FOR ME THERE.
KAHUNA TEAM...
...YOU CAPTURE THE NEW PONI ISLAND KAHUNA HAPU AND BRING HER TO THE ALTAR.
IF SHE RESISTS, DON'T HESITATE TO USE FORCE.

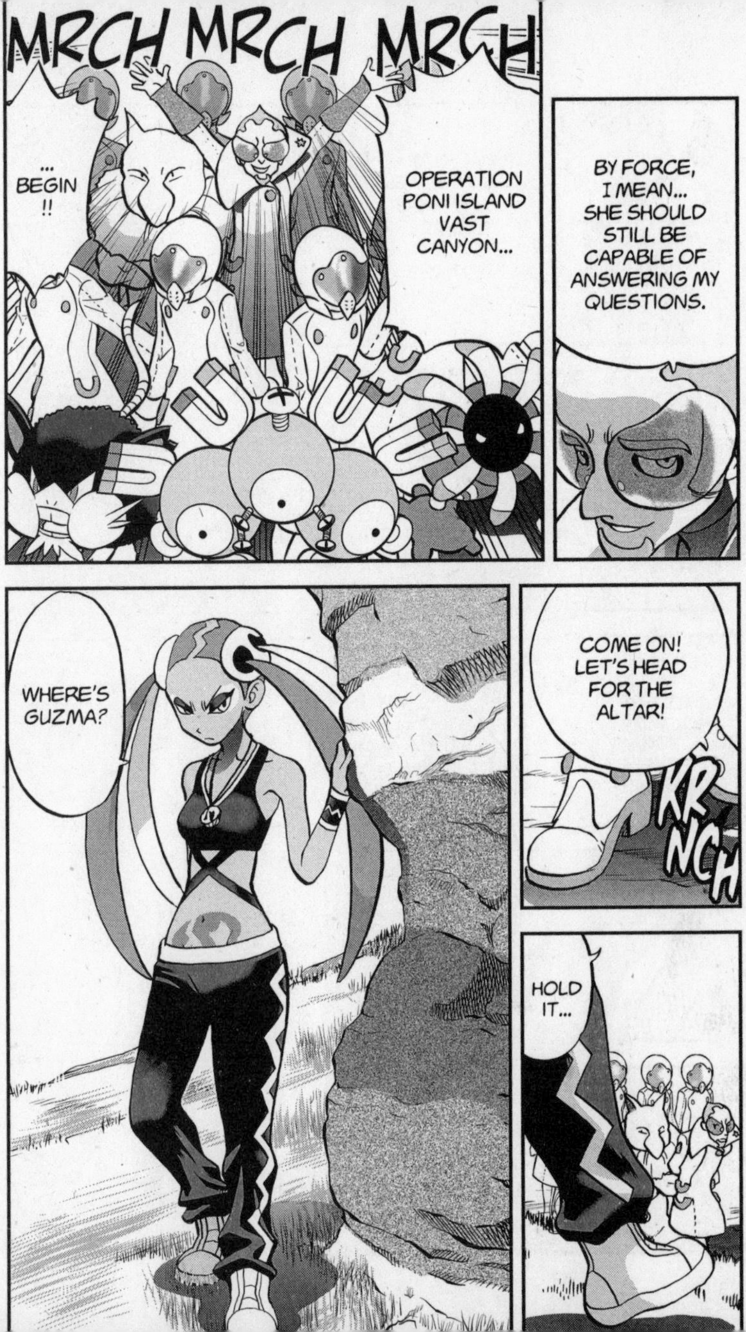
BY FORCE, I MEAN... SHE SHOULD STILL BE CAPABLE OF ANSWERING MY QUESTIONS.
MRCH MRCH MRCH
OPERATION PONI ISLAND VAST CANYON...
... BEGIN !!
COME ON! LET'S HEAD FOR THE ALTAR!
KRNCH
HOLD IT...
WHERE'S GUZMA?

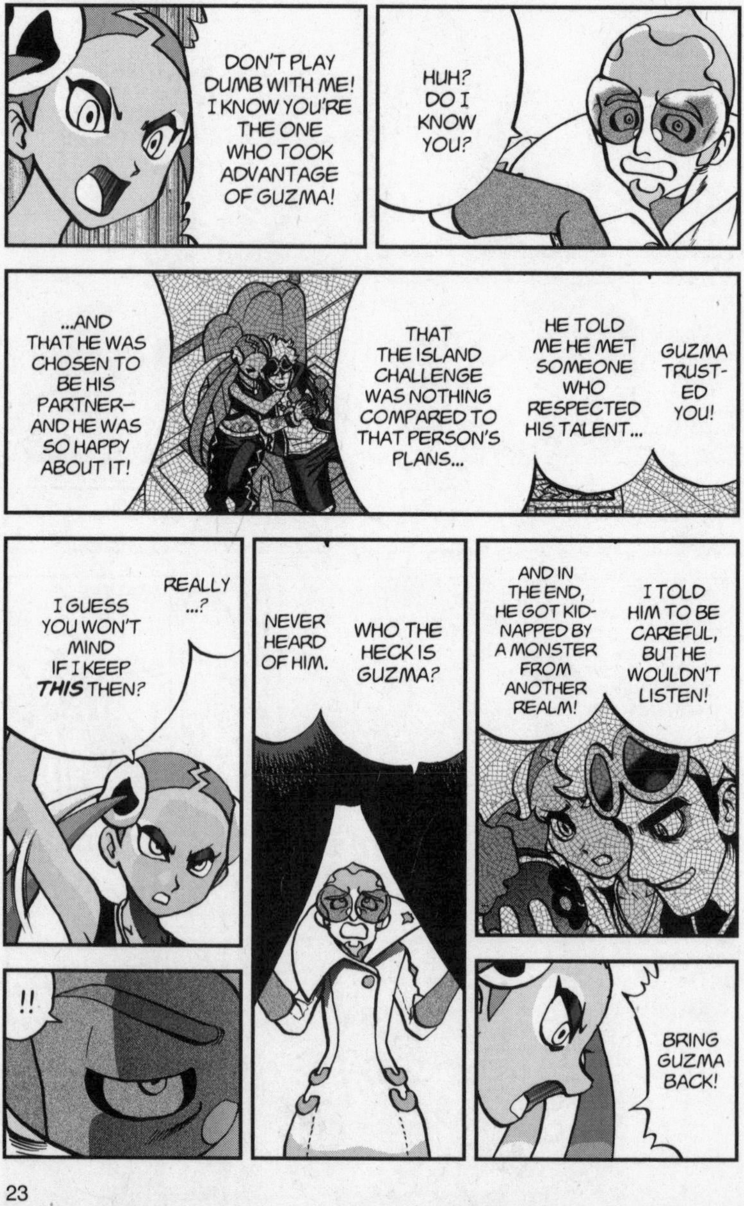
HUH? DO I KNOW YOU?
DON'T PLAY DUMB WITH ME! I KNOW YOU'RE THE ONE WHO TOOK ADVANTAGE OF GUZMA!
GUZMA TRUST-ED YOU!
HE TOLD ME HE MET SOMEONE WHO RESPECTED HIS TALENT...
THAT THE ISLAND CHALLENGE WAS NOTHING COMPARED TO THAT PERSON'S PLANS...
...AND THAT HE WAS CHOSEN TO BE HIS PARTNER—AND HE WAS SO HAPPY ABOUT IT!
I TOLD HIM TO BE CAREFUL, BUT HE WOULDN'T LISTEN!
AND IN THE END, HE GOT KID-NAPPED BY A MONSTER FROM ANOTHER REALM!
BRING GUZMA BACK!
WHO THE HECK IS GUZMA?
NEVER HEARD OF HIM.
REALLY ...?
I GUESS YOU WON'T MIND IF I KEEP ***THIS*** THEN?
!!

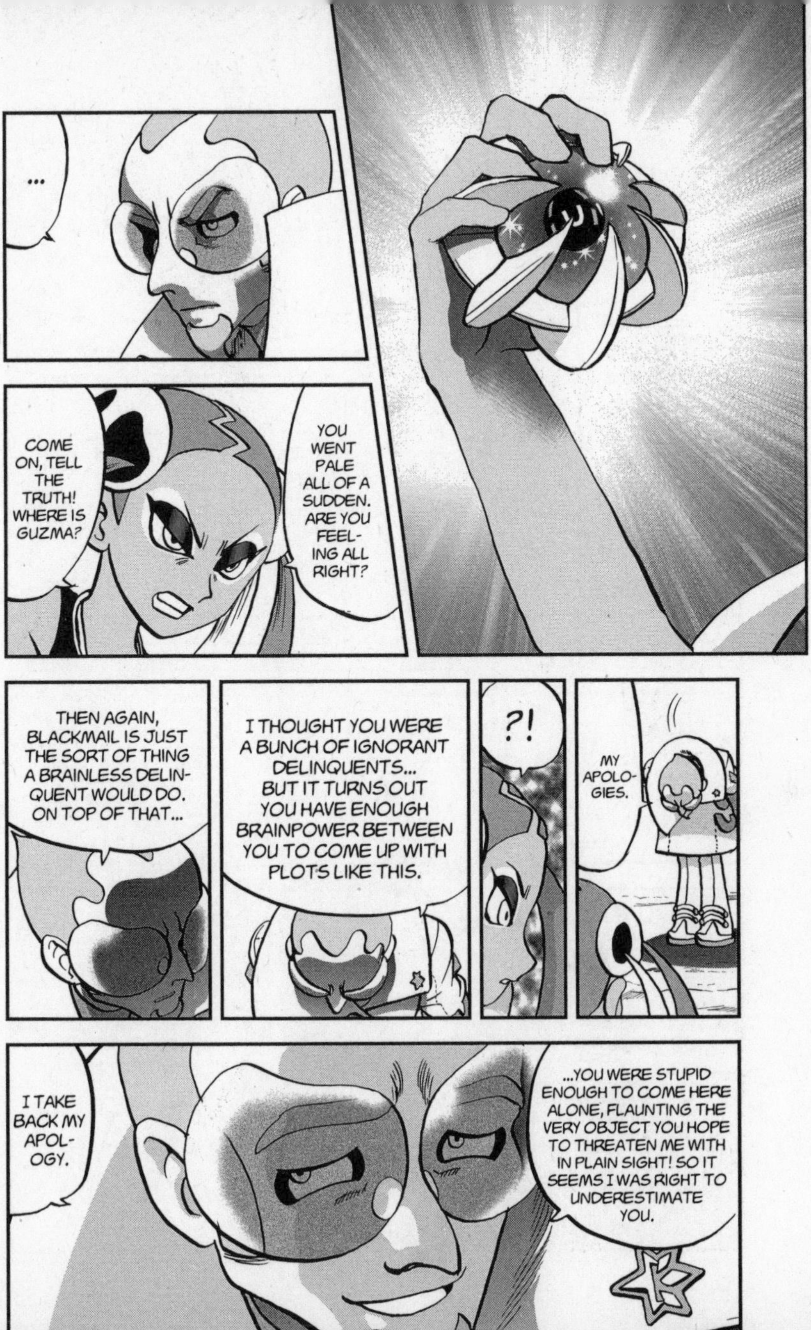
...
YOU WENT PALE ALL OF A SUDDEN. ARE YOU FEEL-ING ALL RIGHT?
COME ON, TELL THE TRUTH! WHERE IS GUZMA?
MY APOLO-GIES.
?!
I THOUGHT YOU WERE A BUNCH OF IGNORANT DELINQUENTS... BUT IT TURNS OUT YOU HAVE ENOUGH BRAINPOWER BETWEEN YOU TO COME UP WITH PLOTS LIKE THIS.
THEN AGAIN, BLACKMAIL IS JUST THE SORT OF THING A BRAINLESS DELIN-QUENT WOULD DO. ON TOP OF THAT...
...YOU WERE STUPID ENOUGH TO COME HERE ALONE, FLAUNTING THE VERY OBJECT YOU HOPE TO THREATEN ME WITH IN PLAIN SIGHT! SO IT SEEMS I WAS RIGHT TO UNDERESTIMATE YOU.
I TAKE BACK MY APOL-OGY.

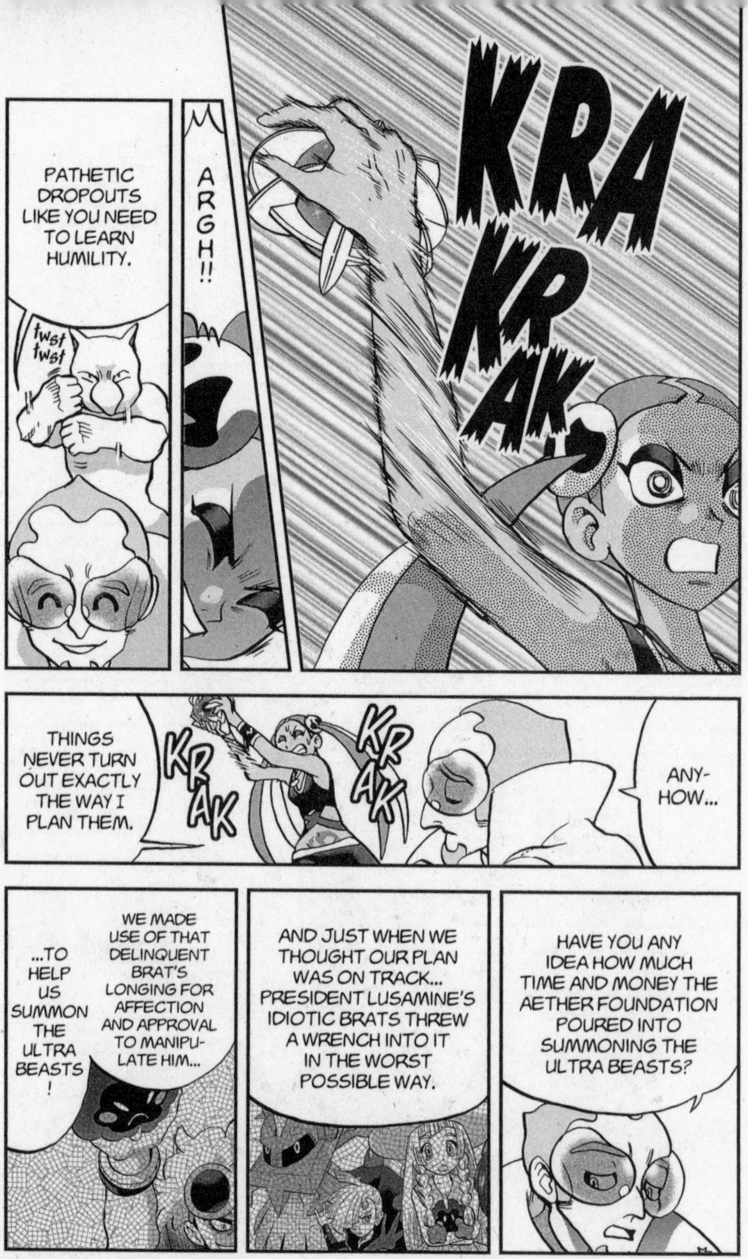
KRA KRAK
ARGH!!
PATHETIC DROPOUTS LIKE YOU NEED TO LEARN HUMILITY.
twst twst
ANY-HOW...
KRAK
KRAK
THINGS NEVER TURN OUT EXACTLY THE WAY I PLAN THEM.
HAVE YOU ANY IDEA HOW MUCH TIME AND MONEY THE AETHER FOUNDATION POURED INTO SUMMONING THE ULTRA BEASTS?
AND JUST WHEN WE THOUGHT OUR PLAN WAS ON TRACK... PRESIDENT LUSAMINE'S IDIOTIC BRATS THREW A WRENCH INTO IT IN THE WORST POSSIBLE WAY.
WE MADE USE OF THAT DELINQUENT BRAT'S LONGING FOR AFFECTION AND APPROVAL TO MANIPULATE HIM...
...TO HELP US SUMMON THE ULTRA BEASTS!

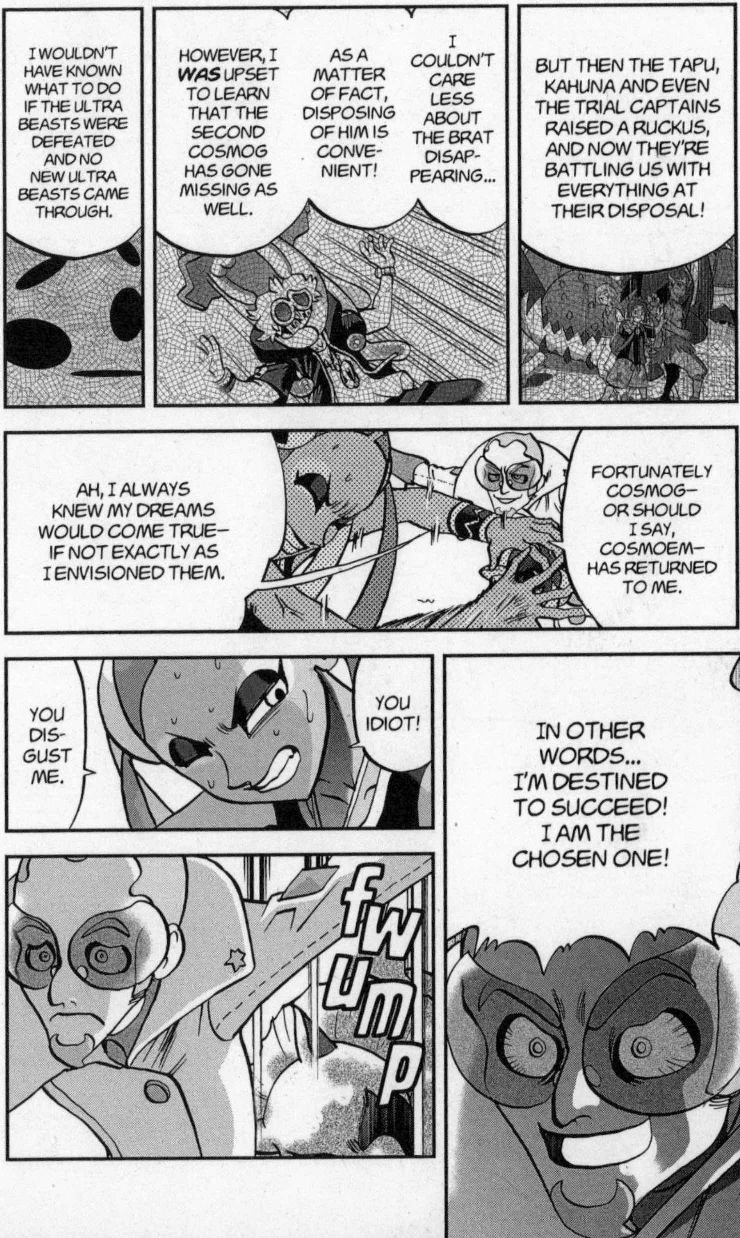
BUT THEN THE TAPU, KAHUNA AND EVEN THE TRIAL CAPTAINS RAISED A RUCKUS, AND NOW THEY'RE BATTLING US WITH EVERYTHING AT THEIR DISPOSAL!
I COULDN'T CARE LESS ABOUT THE BRAT DISAPPEARING...
AS A MATTER OF FACT, DISPOSING OF HIM IS CONVENIENT!
HOWEVER, I **WAS** UPSET TO LEARN THAT THE SECOND COSMOG HAS GONE MISSING AS WELL.
I WOULDN'T HAVE KNOWN WHAT TO DO IF THE ULTRA BEASTS WERE DEFEATED AND NO NEW ULTRA BEASTS CAME THROUGH.
FORTUNATELY COSMOG—OR SHOULD I SAY, COSMOEM—HAS RETURNED TO ME.
AH, I ALWAYS KNEW MY DREAMS WOULD COME TRUE—IF NOT EXACTLY AS I ENVISIONED THEM.
IN OTHER WORDS... I'M DESTINED TO SUCCEED! I AM THE CHOSEN ONE!
YOU IDIOT!
YOU DISGUST ME.
fwump

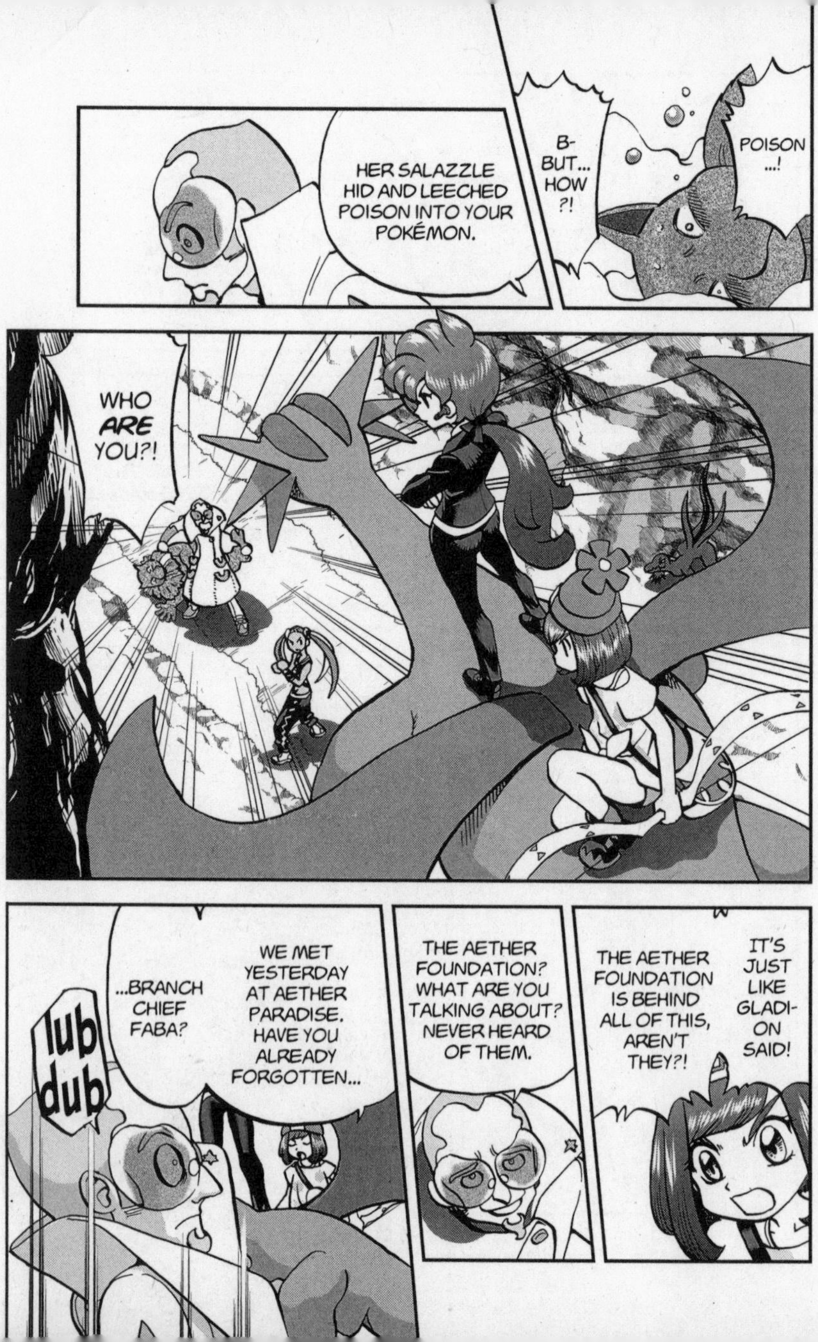
POISON ...!
B- BUT... HOW ?!
HER SALAZZLE HID AND LEECHED POISON INTO YOUR POKÉMON.
WHO ARE YOU?!
IT'S JUST LIKE GLADI- ON SAID!
THE AETHER FOUNDATION IS BEHIND ALL OF THIS, AREN'T THEY?!
THE AETHER FOUNDATION? WHAT ARE YOU TALKING ABOUT? NEVER HEARD OF THEM.
WE MET YESTERDAY AT AETHER PARADISE. HAVE YOU ALREADY FORGOTTEN...
...BRANCH CHIEF FABA?
lub dub

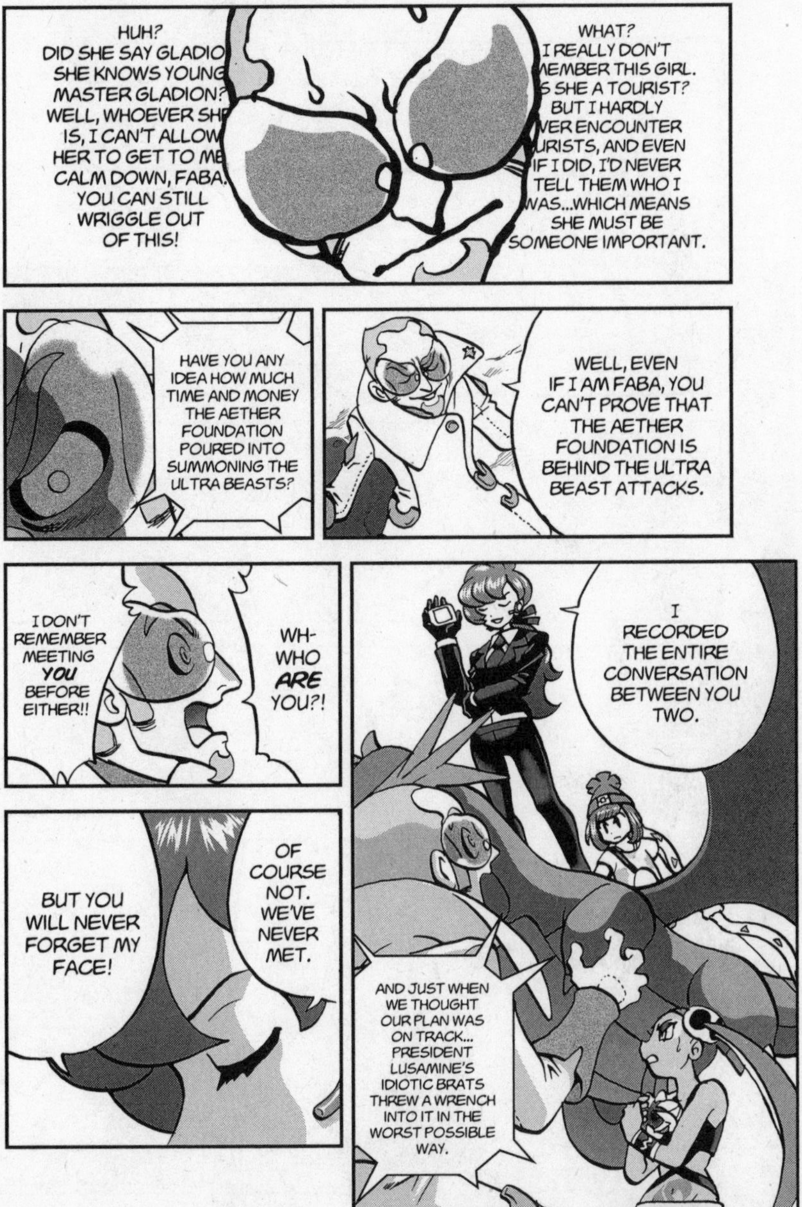
WHAT? I REALLY DON'T EMEMBER THIS GIRL. S SHE A TOURIST? BUT I HARDLY VER ENCOUNTER URISTS, AND EVEN IF I DID, I'D NEVER TELL THEM WHO I WAS...WHICH MEANS SHE MUST BE SOMEONE IMPORTANT.
HUH? DID SHE SAY GLADIO SHE KNOWS YOUNG MASTER GLADION? WELL, WHOEVER SH IS, I CAN'T ALLOW HER TO GET TO ME CALM DOWN, FABA. YOU CAN STILL WRIGGLE OUT OF THIS!
WELL, EVEN IF I AM FABA, YOU CAN'T PROVE THAT THE AETHER FOUNDATION IS BEHIND THE ULTRA BEAST ATTACKS.
HAVE YOU ANY IDEA HOW MUCH TIME AND MONEY THE AETHER FOUNDATION POURED INTO SUMMONING THE ULTRA BEASTS?
I RECORDED THE ENTIRE CONVERSATION BETWEEN YOU TWO.
AND JUST WHEN WE THOUGHT OUR PLAN WAS ON TRACK... PRESIDENT LUSAMINE'S IDIOTIC BRATS THREW A WRENCH INTO IT IN THE WORST POSSIBLE WAY.
WH- WHO ***ARE*** YOU?!
I DON'T REMEMBER MEETING ***YOU*** BEFORE EITHER!!
OF COURSE NOT. WE'VE NEVER MET.
BUT YOU WILL NEVER FORGET MY FACE!

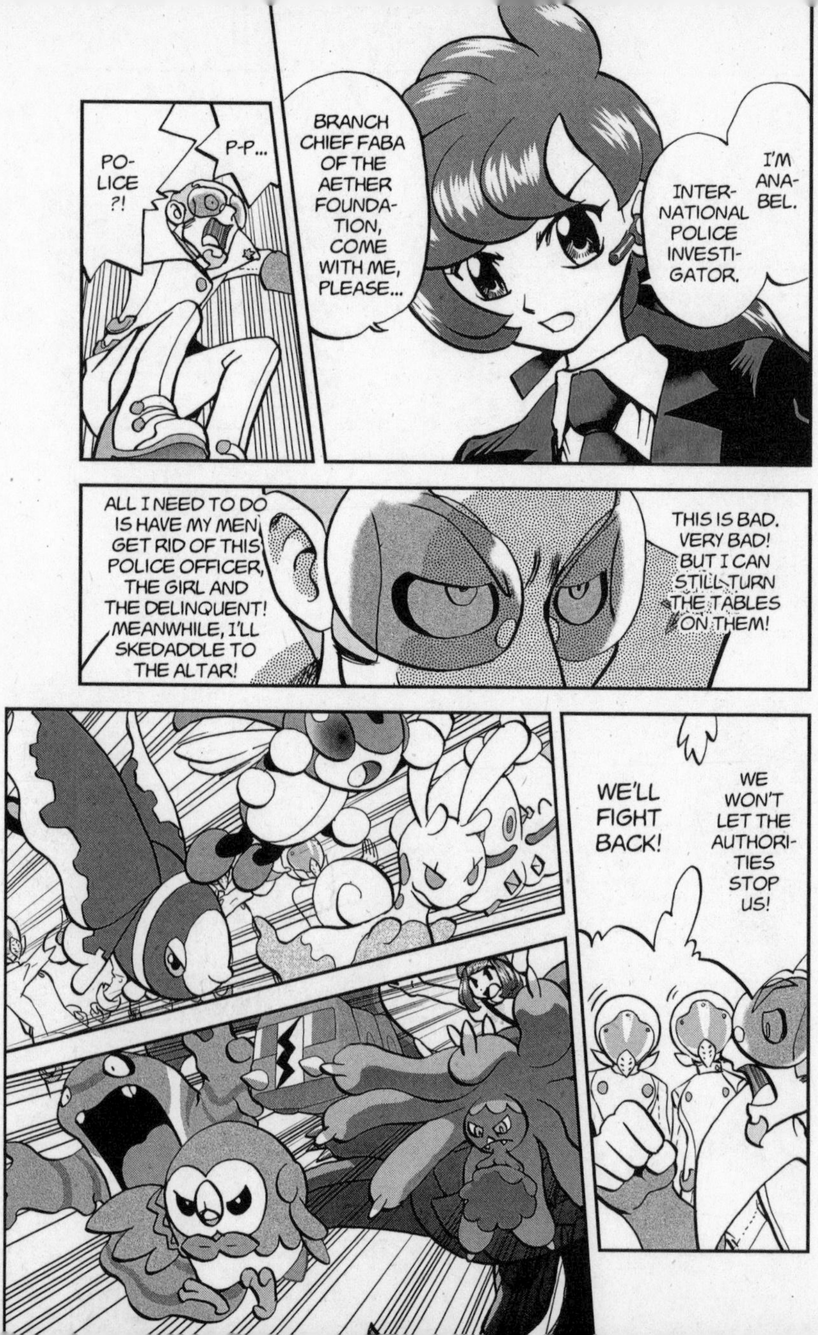
I'M ANA-BEL.
INTER-NATIONAL POLICE INVESTI-GATOR.
BRANCH CHIEF FABA OF THE AETHER FOUNDA-TION, COME WITH ME, PLEASE...
P-P...
PO-LICE ?!
THIS IS BAD. VERY BAD! BUT I CAN STILL TURN THE TABLES ON THEM!
ALL I NEED TO DO IS HAVE MY MEN GET RID OF THIS POLICE OFFICER, THE GIRL AND THE DELINQUENT! MEANWHILE, I'LL SKEDADDLE TO THE ALTAR!
WE WON'T LET THE AUTHORI-TIES STOP US!
WE'LL FIGHT BACK!

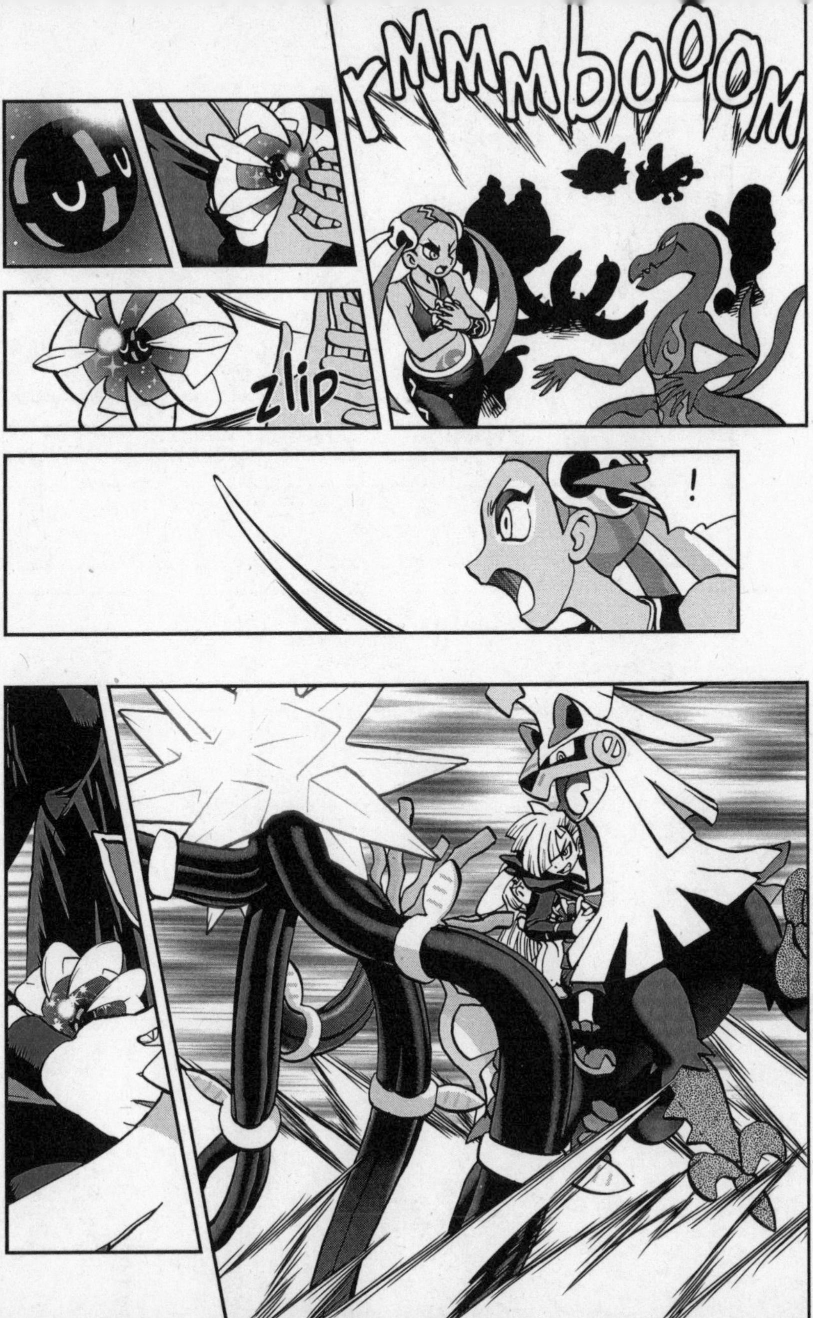
rMMMbOOOM
zlip
!

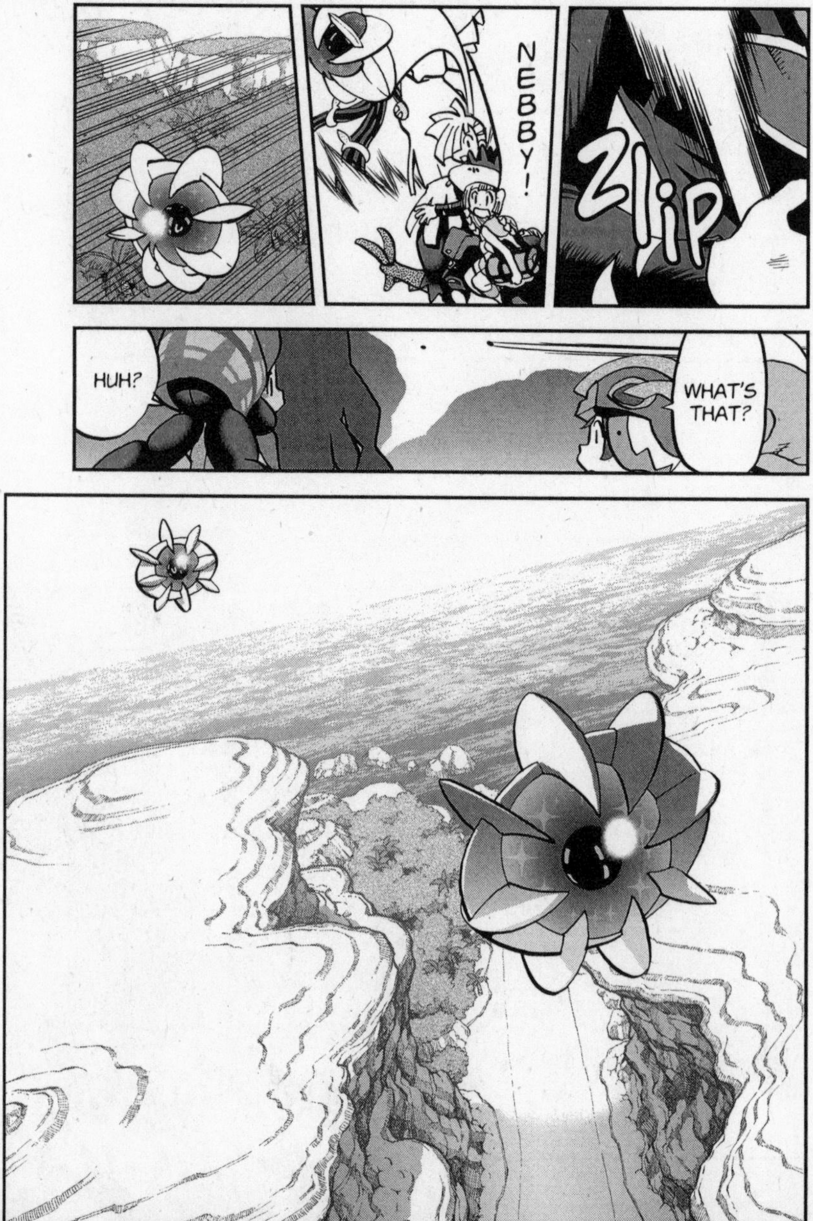
ZLIP
NEBBY!
WHAT'S THAT?
HUH?

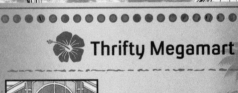

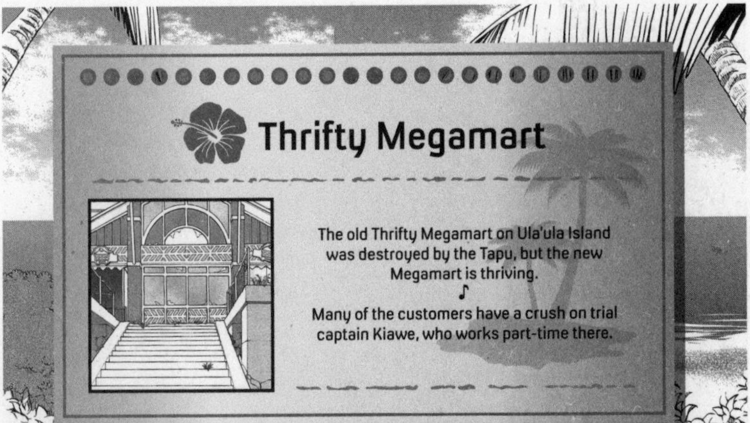

Thrifty Megamart

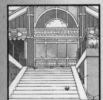

The old Thrifty Megamart on Ula'ula Island
was destroyed by the Tapu, but the new
Megamart is thriving.
♪
Many of the customers have a crush on trial
captain Kiawe, who works part-time there.

Guide to Alola 20

Adventure 24
Play the Melody That Echoes in the Altar

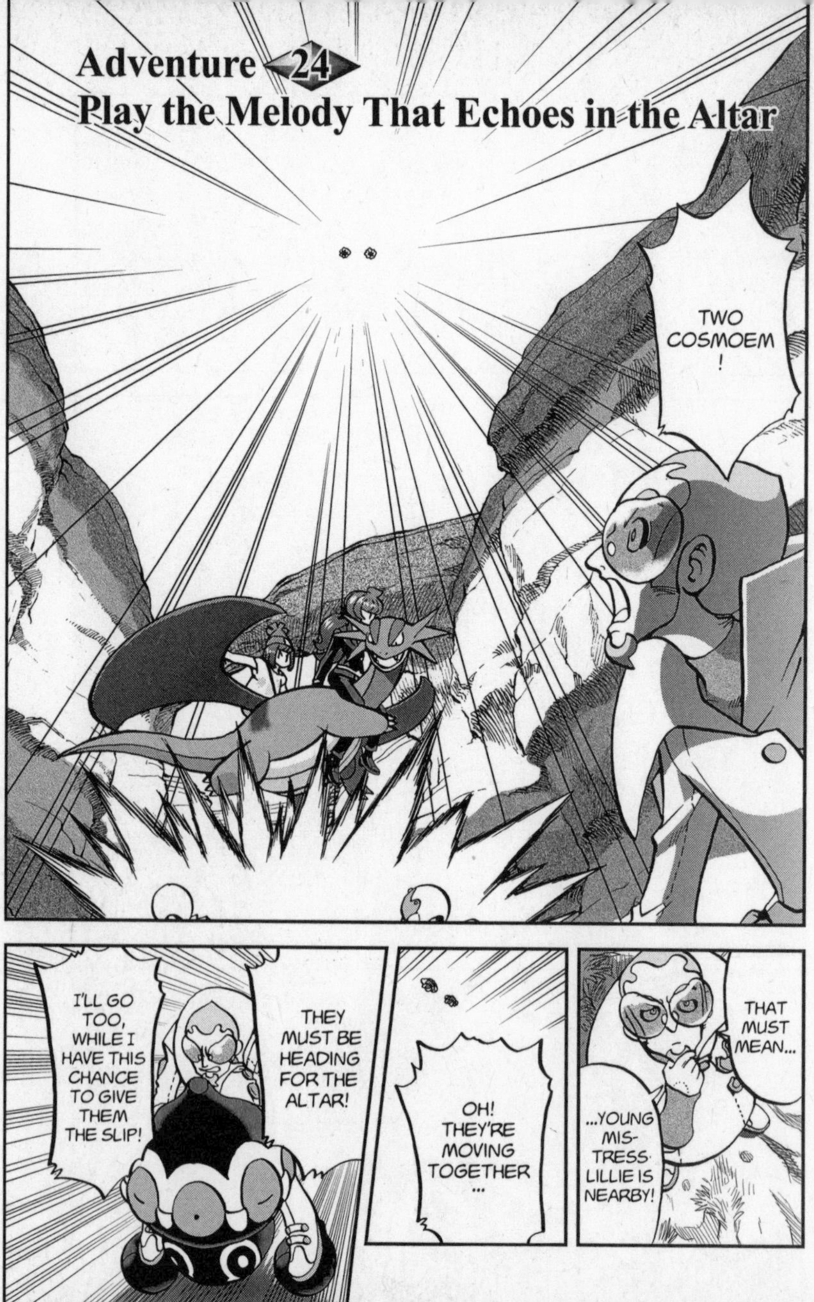

TWO COSMOEM !
THAT MUST MEAN...
...YOUNG MIS-TRESS LILLIE IS NEARBY!
OH! THEY'RE MOVING TOGETHER ...
THEY MUST BE HEADING FOR THE ALTAR!
I'LL GO TOO, WHILE I HAVE THIS CHANCE TO GIVE THEM THE SLIP!

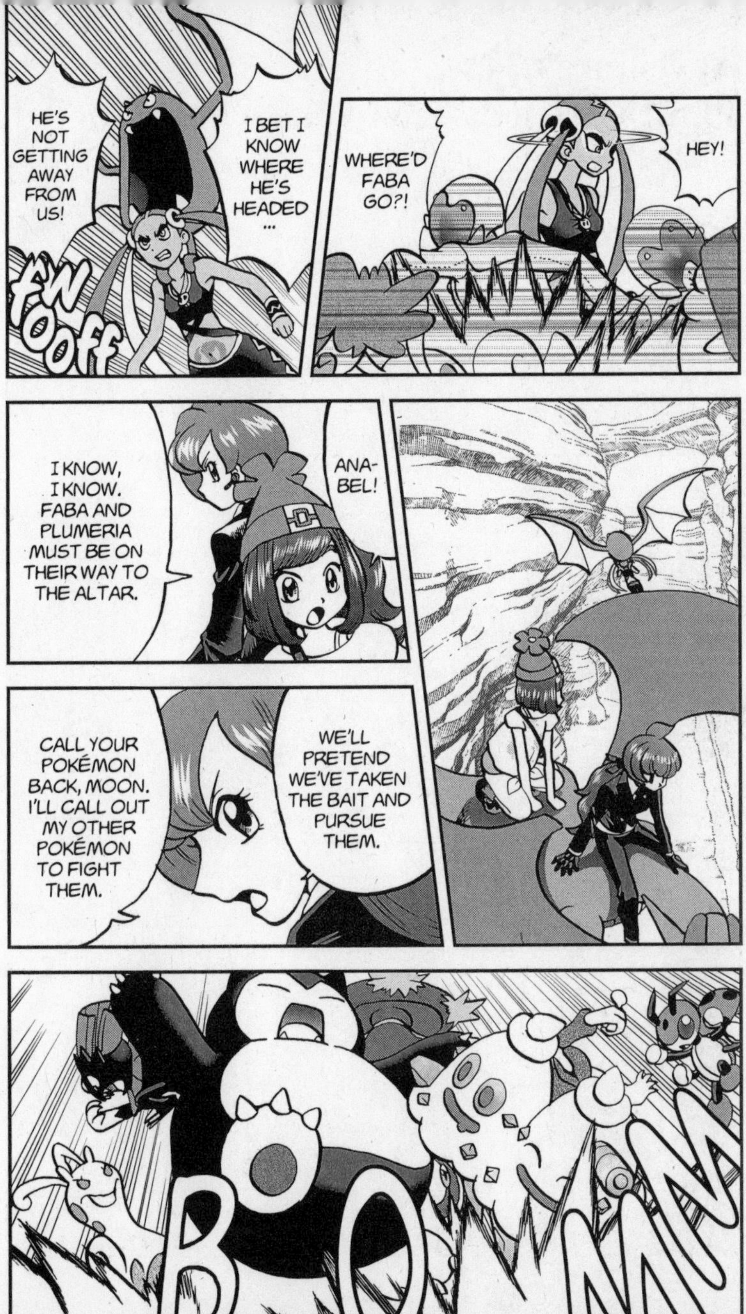
HEY!
WHERE'D FABA GO?!
I BET I KNOW WHERE HE'S HEADED...
HE'S NOT GETTING AWAY FROM US!
FWOOFF
ANA-BEL!
I KNOW, I KNOW. FABA AND PLUMERIA MUST BE ON THEIR WAY TO THE ALTAR.
WE'LL PRETEND WE'VE TAKEN THE BAIT AND PURSUE THEM.
CALL YOUR POKÉMON BACK, MOON. I'LL CALL OUT MY OTHER POKÉMON TO FIGHT THEM.
BOOMM

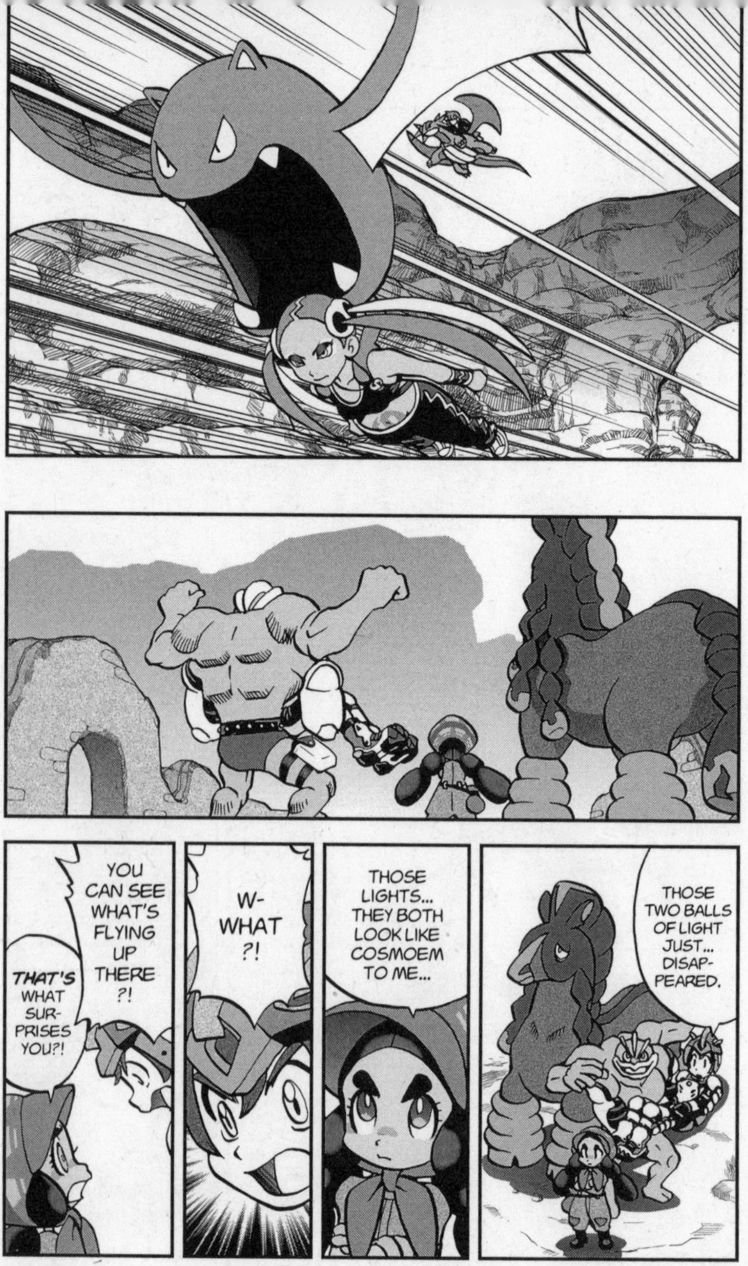
THOSE TWO BALLS OF LIGHT JUST... DISAPPEARED.
THOSE LIGHTS... THEY BOTH LOOK LIKE COSMOEM TO ME...
W-WHAT?!
YOU CAN SEE WHAT'S FLYING UP THERE?!
THAT'S WHAT SURPRISES YOU?!

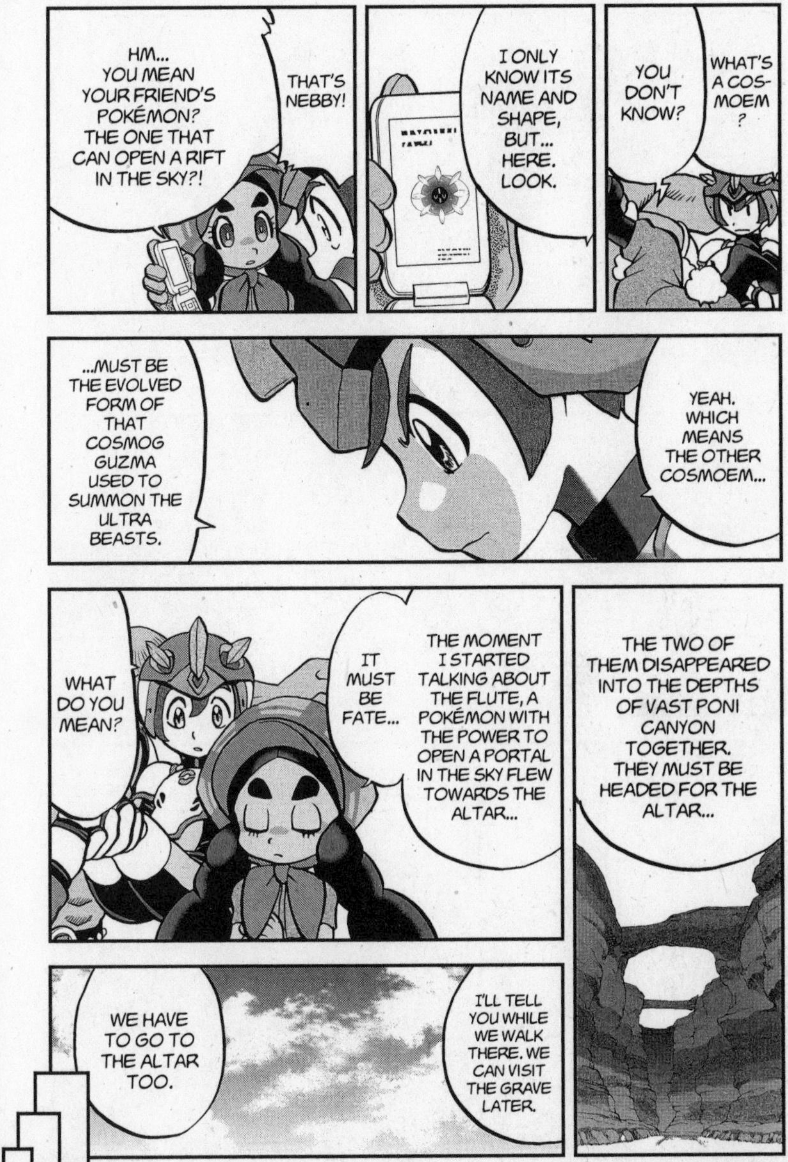
WHAT'S A COS-MOEM?
YOU DON'T KNOW?
I ONLY KNOW ITS NAME AND SHAPE, BUT... HERE. LOOK.
THAT'S NEBBY!
HM... YOU MEAN YOUR FRIEND'S POKÉMON? THE ONE THAT CAN OPEN A RIFT IN THE SKY?!
YEAH. WHICH MEANS THE OTHER COSMOEM...
...MUST BE THE EVOLVED FORM OF THAT COSMOG GUZMA USED TO SUMMON THE ULTRA BEASTS.
THE TWO OF THEM DISAPPEARED INTO THE DEPTHS OF VAST PONI CANYON TOGETHER. THEY MUST BE HEADED FOR THE ALTAR...
IT MUST BE FATE... THE MOMENT I STARTED TALKING ABOUT THE FLUTE, A POKÉMON WITH THE POWER TO OPEN A PORTAL IN THE SKY FLEW TOWARDS THE ALTAR...
WHAT DO YOU MEAN?
I'LL TELL YOU WHILE WE WALK THERE. WE CAN VISIT THE GRAVE LATER.
WE HAVE TO GO TO THE ALTAR TOO.

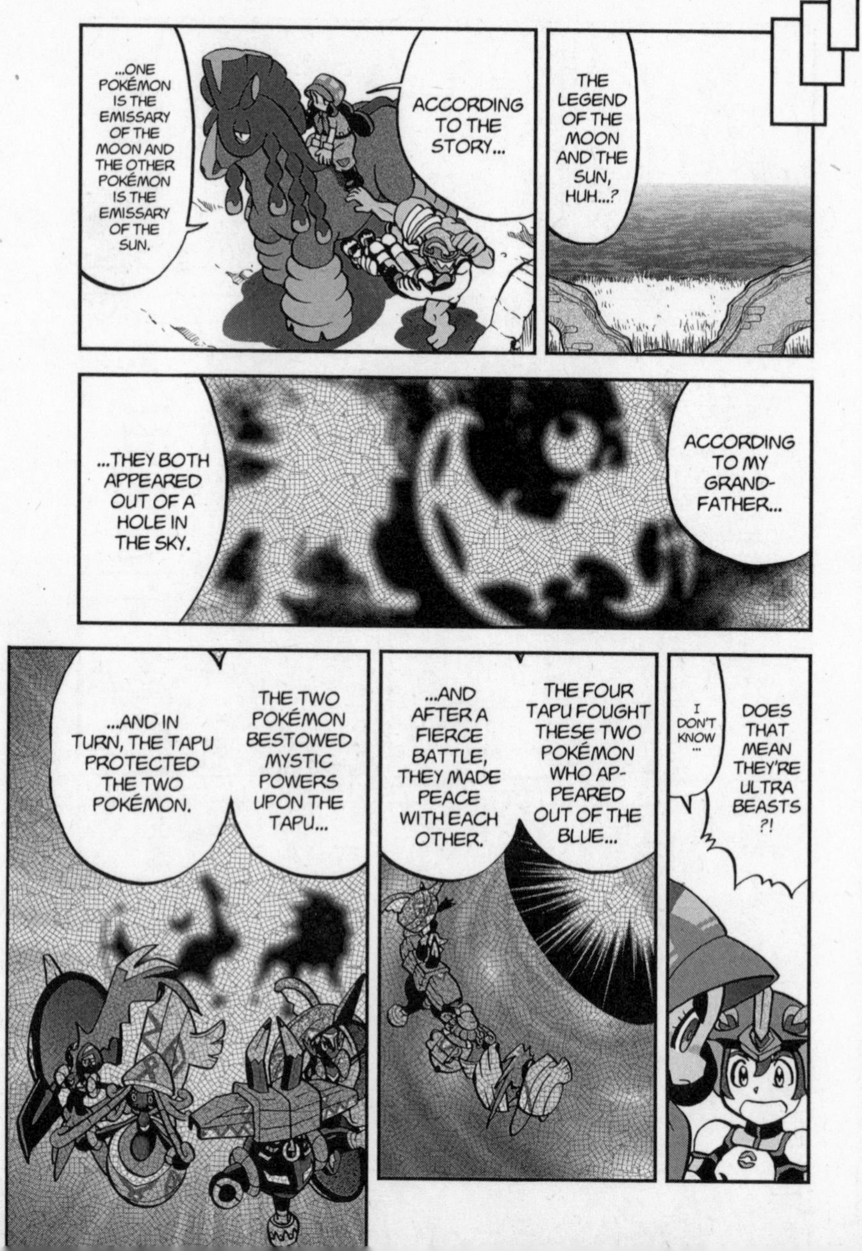
THE LEGEND OF THE MOON AND THE SUN, HUH...?
ACCORDING TO THE STORY...
...ONE POKÉMON IS THE EMISSARY OF THE MOON AND THE OTHER POKÉMON IS THE EMISSARY OF THE SUN.
ACCORDING TO MY GRANDFATHER...
...THEY BOTH APPEARED OUT OF A HOLE IN THE SKY.
DOES THAT MEAN THEY'RE ULTRA BEASTS?!
I DON'T KNOW...
THE FOUR TAPU FOUGHT THESE TWO POKÉMON WHO APPEARED OUT OF THE BLUE...
...AND AFTER A FIERCE BATTLE, THEY MADE PEACE WITH EACH OTHER.
THE TWO POKÉMON BESTOWED MYSTIC POWERS UPON THE TAPU...
...AND IN TURN, THE TAPU PROTECTED THE TWO POKÉMON.

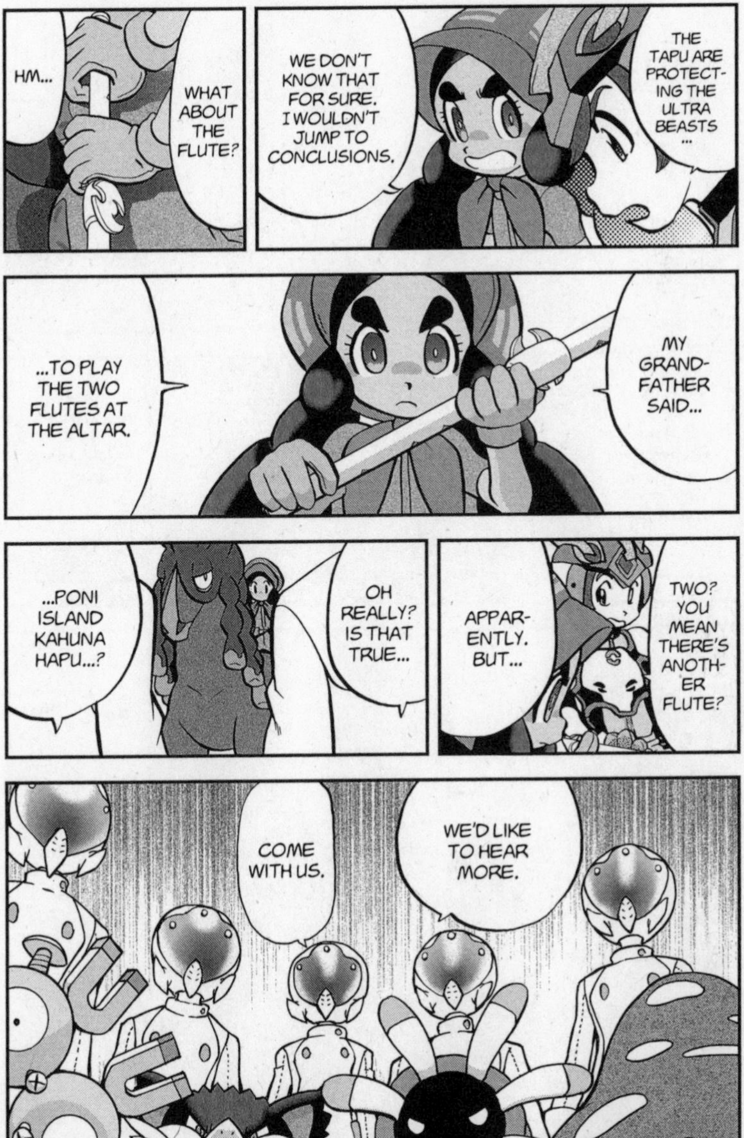
THE TAPU ARE PROTECTING THE ULTRA BEASTS ...
WE DON'T KNOW THAT FOR SURE. I WOULDN'T JUMP TO CONCLUSIONS.
WHAT ABOUT THE FLUTE?
HM...
MY GRANDFATHER SAID...
...TO PLAY THE TWO FLUTES AT THE ALTAR.
TWO? YOU MEAN THERE'S ANOTHER FLUTE?
APPARENTLY. BUT...
OH REALLY? IS THAT TRUE...
...PONI ISLAND KAHUNA HAPU...?
WE'D LIKE TO HEAR MORE.
COME WITH US.

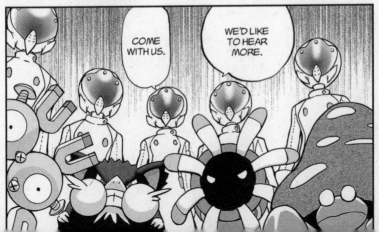

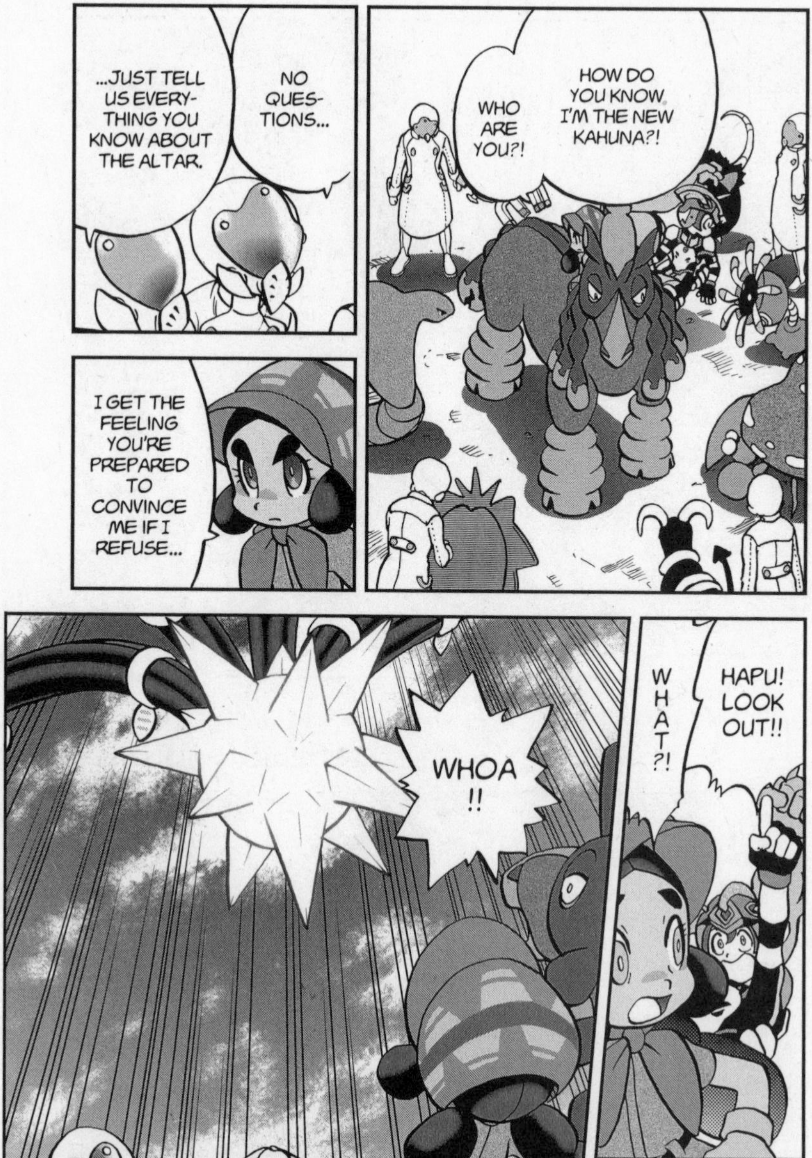
HOW DO YOU KNOW I'M THE NEW KAHUNA?!
WHO ARE YOU?!
NO QUES-TIONS...
...JUST TELL US EVERY-THING YOU KNOW ABOUT THE ALTAR.
I GET THE FEELING YOU'RE PREPARED TO CONVINCE ME IF I REFUSE...
HAPU! LOOK OUT!!
WHAT?!
WHOA !!

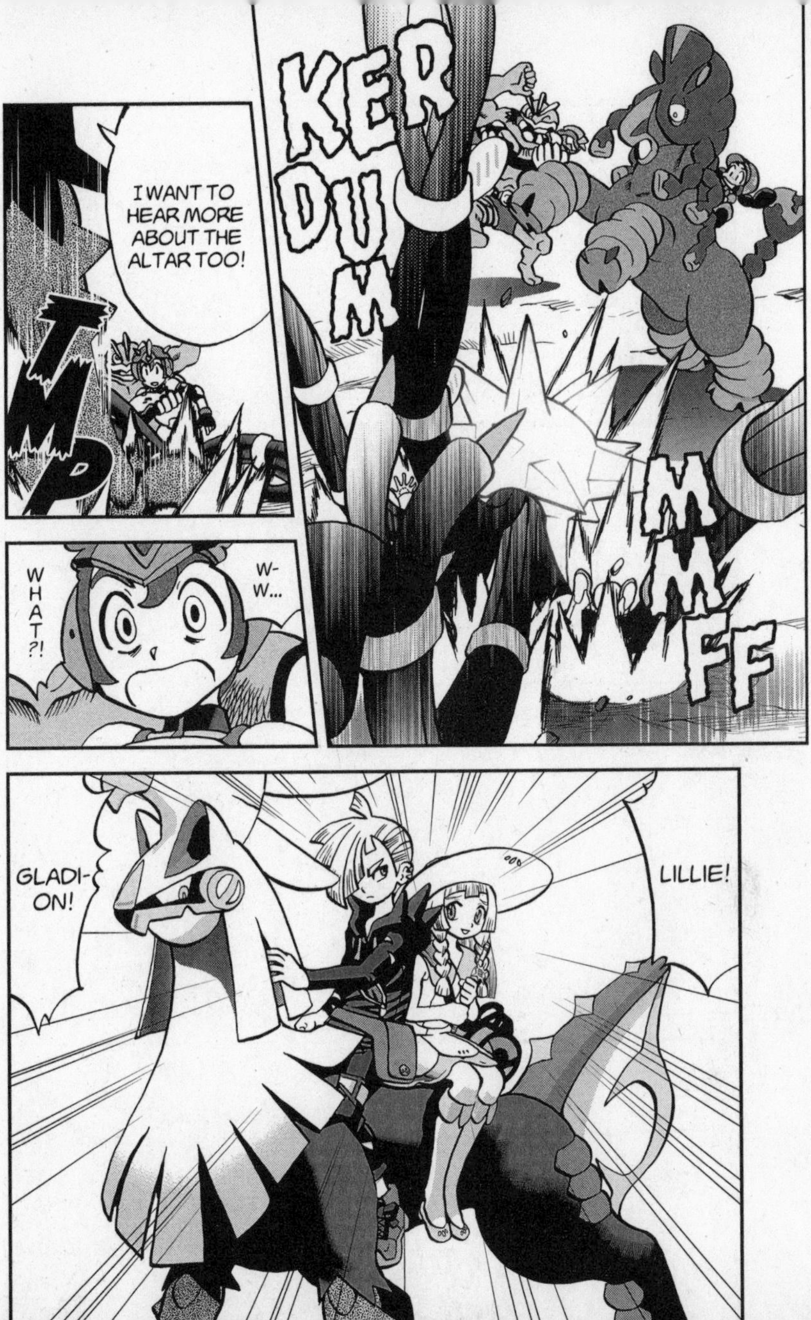
KERDUUM
MMMFF
I WANT TO HEAR MORE ABOUT THE ALTAR TOO!
TMP
W-W...
WHAT?!
LILLIE!
GLADI-ON!

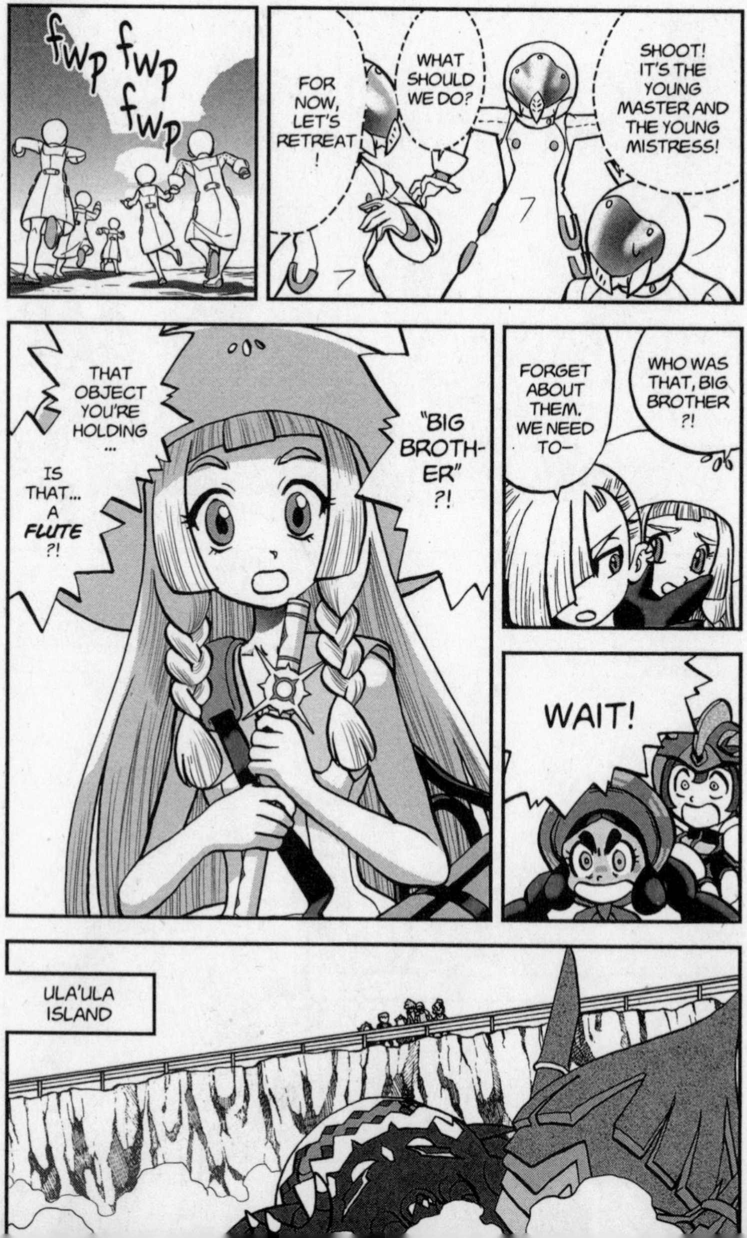
SHOOT! IT'S THE YOUNG MASTER AND THE YOUNG MISTRESS!
WHAT SHOULD WE DO?
FOR NOW, LET'S RETREAT!
fwp fwp fwp
WHO WAS THAT, BIG BROTHER?!
FORGET ABOUT THEM. WE NEED TO–
WAIT!
"BIG BROTHER"?!
THAT OBJECT YOU'RE HOLDING...
IS THAT... A *FLUTE*?!
ULA'ULA ISLAND

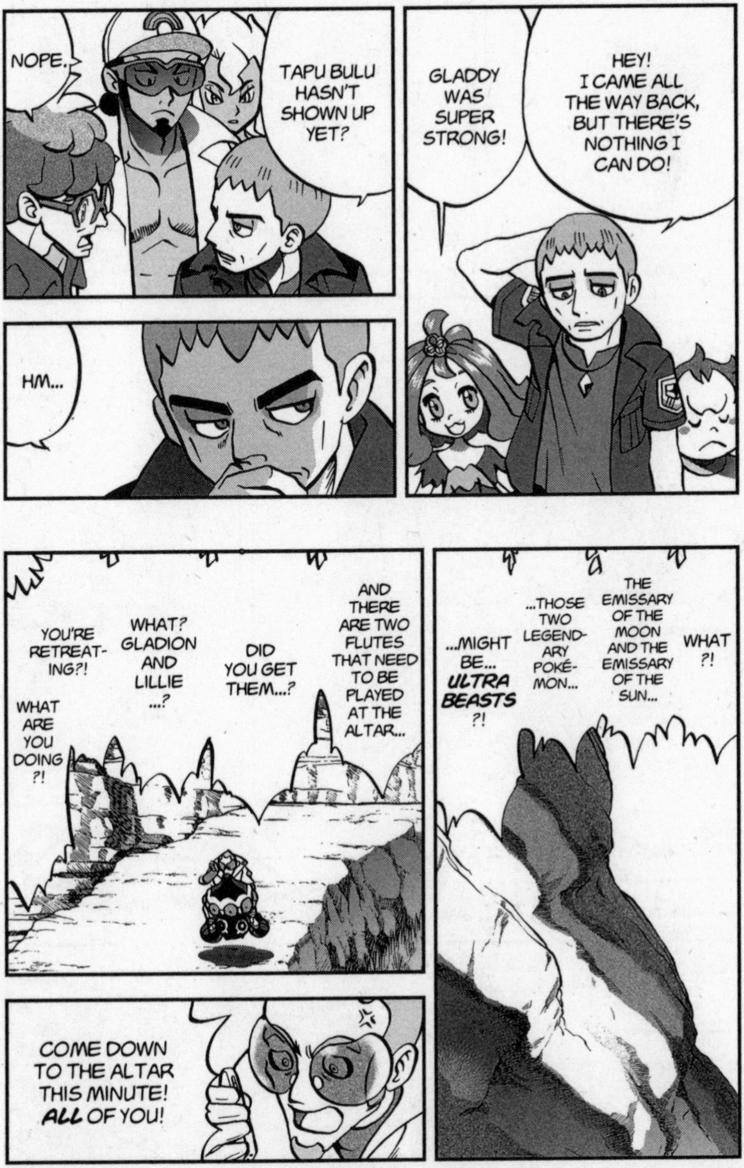
HEY! I CAME ALL THE WAY BACK, BUT THERE'S NOTHING I CAN DO!
GLADDY WAS SUPER STRONG!
TAPU BULU HASN'T SHOWN UP YET?
NOPE.
HM...
WHAT?!
THE EMISSARY OF THE MOON AND THE EMISSARY OF THE SUN...
...THOSE TWO LEGENDARY POKÉMON...
...MIGHT BE... **ULTRA BEASTS**?!
AND THERE ARE TWO FLUTES THAT NEED TO BE PLAYED AT THE ALTAR...
DID YOU GET THEM...?
WHAT? GLADION AND LILLIE...?
YOU'RE RETREATING?!
WHAT ARE YOU DOING?!
COME DOWN TO THE ALTAR THIS MINUTE! **ALL** OF YOU!

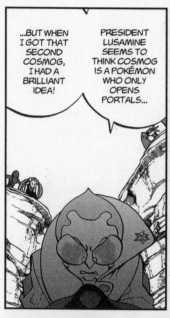

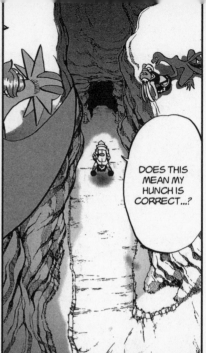

DOES THIS MEAN MY HUNCH IS CORRECT...?
PRESIDENT LUSAMINE SEEMS TO THINK COSMOG IS A POKÉMON WHO ONLY OPENS PORTALS...
...BUT WHEN I GOT THAT SECOND COSMOG, I HAD A BRILLIANT IDEA!
THE LEGENDARY POKÉMON OF THE MOON AND SUN...
...COULD COSMOG BE RELATED TO THEM SOME-HOW?!
I'LL DECIPHER THE SECRET OF THE LEGEND TO ACQUIRE THOSE TWO LEGENDARY POKÉMON AND USE THEM TO CONTROL THE ULTRA BEASTS!
THEN I'LL NO LONGER HAVE TO GO ALONG WITH PRESIDENT LUSAMINE'S FOOLISH OBSESSION WITH CREATING A PARADISE FOR ULTRA BEASTS.

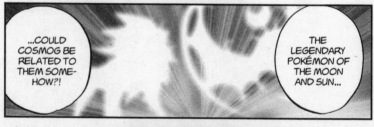

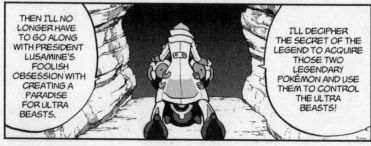

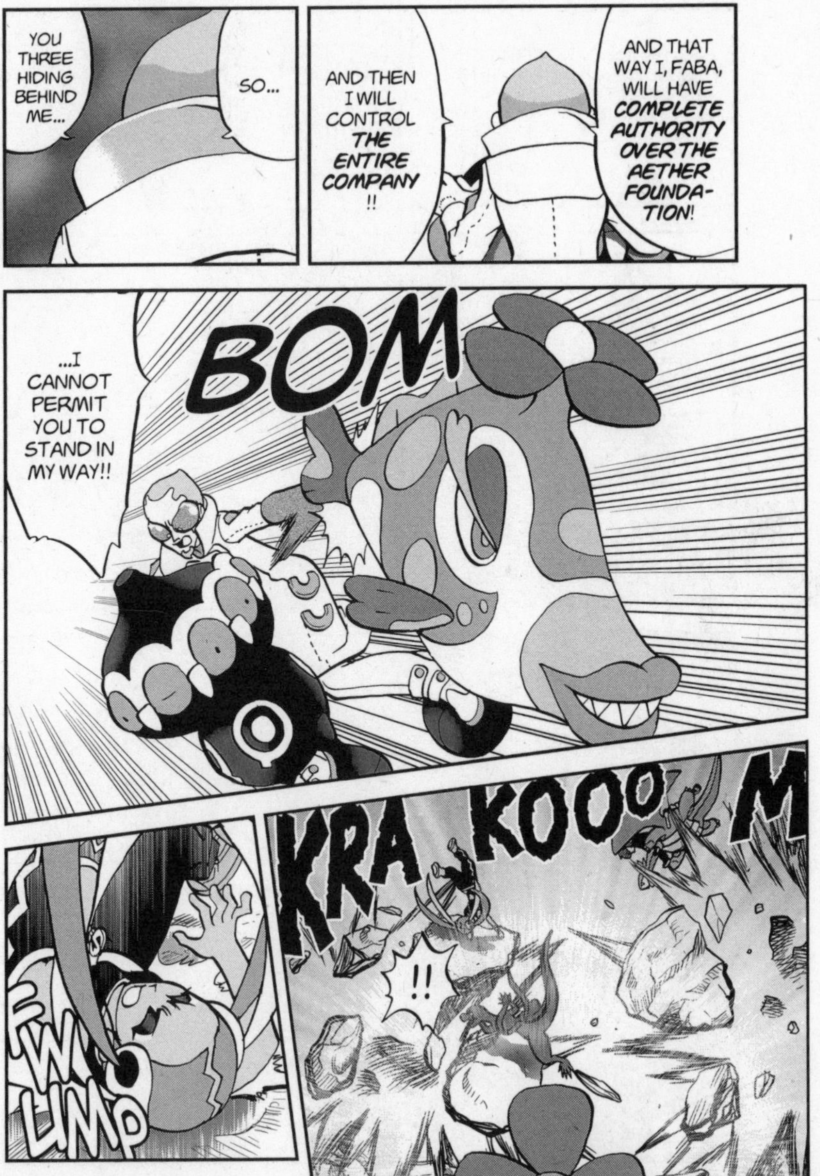
AND THAT WAY I, FABA, WILL HAVE COMPLETE AUTHORITY OVER THE AETHER FOUNDATION!
AND THEN I WILL CONTROL THE ENTIRE COMPANY !!
SO...
YOU THREE HIDING BEHIND ME...
BOM
...I CANNOT PERMIT YOU TO STAND IN MY WAY!!
KRA KOOOM
!!
LUMP

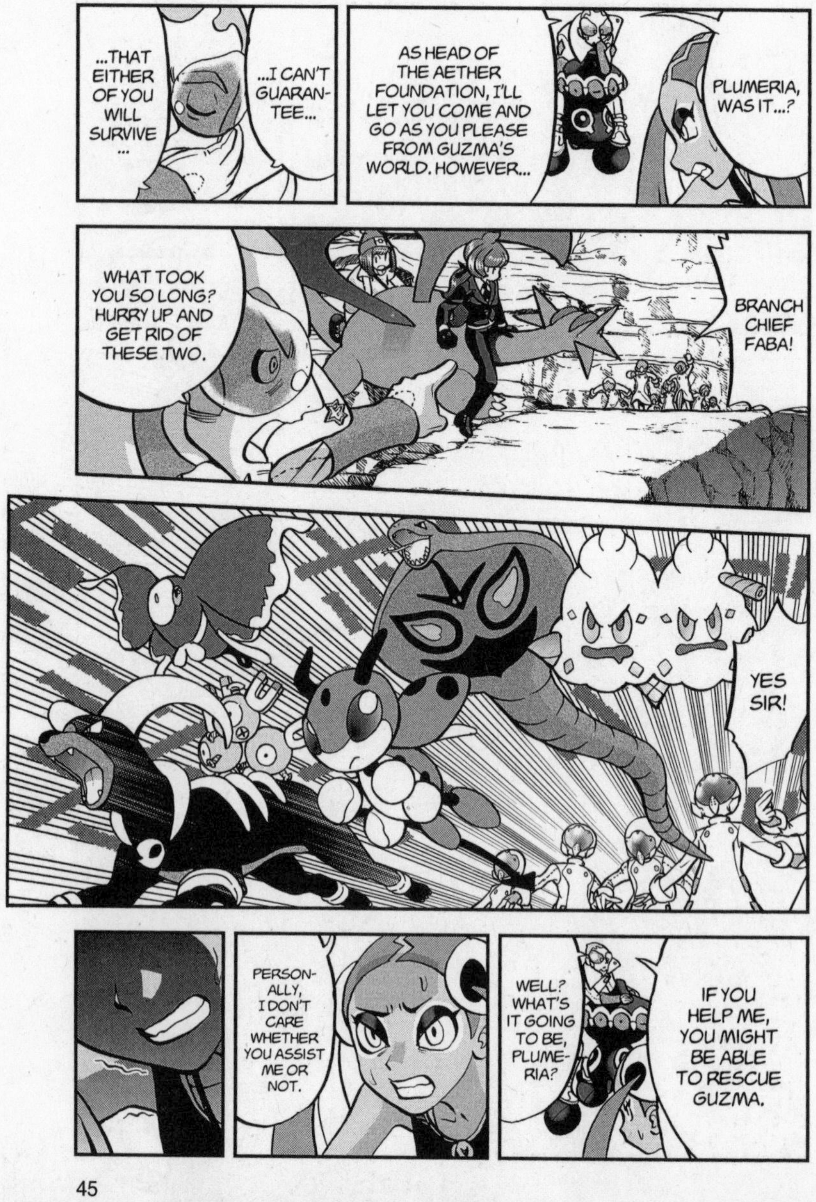
PLUMERIA, WAS IT...?
AS HEAD OF THE AETHER FOUNDATION, I'LL LET YOU COME AND GO AS YOU PLEASE FROM GUZMA'S WORLD. HOWEVER...
...I CAN'T GUARAN- TEE...
...THAT EITHER OF YOU WILL SURVIVE ...
BRANCH CHIEF FABA!
WHAT TOOK YOU SO LONG? HURRY UP AND GET RID OF THESE TWO.
YES SIR!
IF YOU HELP ME, YOU MIGHT BE ABLE TO RESCUE GUZMA.
WELL? WHAT'S IT GOING TO BE, PLUME- RIA?
PERSON- ALLY, I DON'T CARE WHETHER YOU ASSIST ME OR NOT.

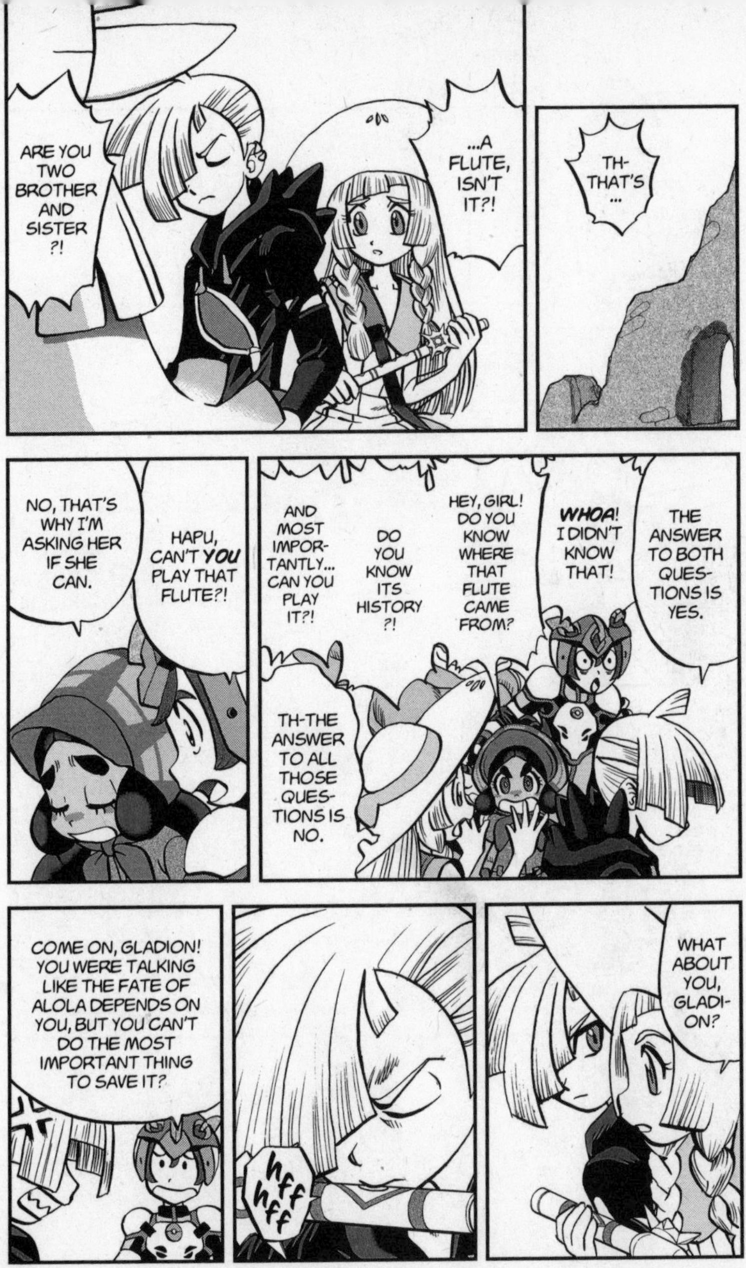
TH-THAT'S ...
...A FLUTE, ISN'T IT?!
ARE YOU TWO BROTHER AND SISTER?!
THE ANSWER TO BOTH QUESTIONS IS YES.
WHOA! I DIDN'T KNOW THAT!
HEY, GIRL! DO YOU KNOW WHERE THAT FLUTE CAME FROM?
DO YOU KNOW ITS HISTORY?!
AND MOST IMPORTANTLY... CAN YOU PLAY IT?!
TH-THE ANSWER TO ALL THOSE QUESTIONS IS NO.
HAPU, CAN'T YOU PLAY THAT FLUTE?!
NO, THAT'S WHY I'M ASKING HER IF SHE CAN.
WHAT ABOUT YOU, GLADION?
hff hff
COME ON, GLADION! YOU WERE TALKING LIKE THE FATE OF ALOLA DEPENDS ON YOU, BUT YOU CAN'T DO THE MOST IMPORTANT THING TO SAVE IT?

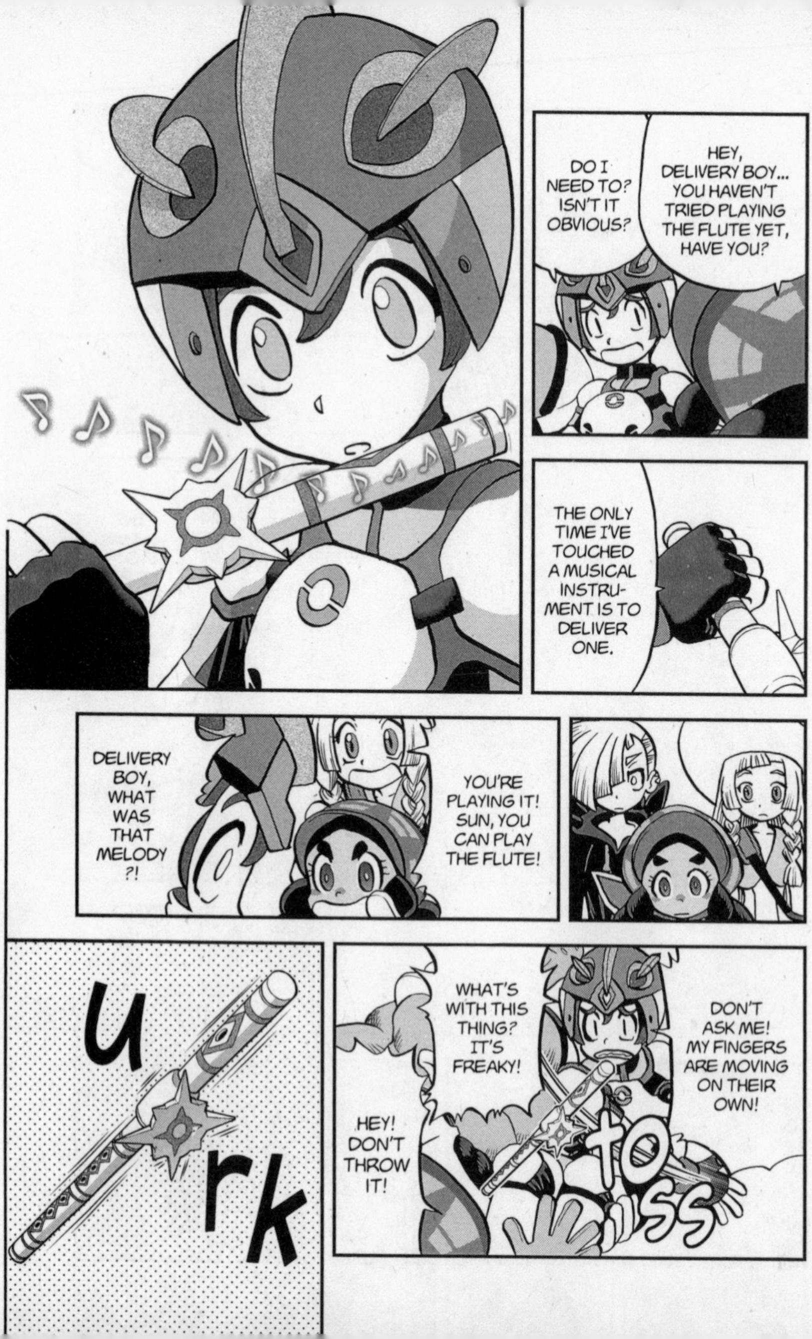
HEY, DELIVERY BOY... YOU HAVEN'T TRIED PLAYING THE FLUTE YET, HAVE YOU?
DO I NEED TO? ISN'T IT OBVIOUS?
THE ONLY TIME I'VE TOUCHED A MUSICAL INSTRU-MENT IS TO DELIVER ONE.
YOU'RE PLAYING IT! SUN, YOU CAN PLAY THE FLUTE!
DELIVERY BOY, WHAT WAS THAT MELODY?!
DON'T ASK ME! MY FINGERS ARE MOVING ON THEIR OWN!
WHAT'S WITH THIS THING? IT'S FREAKY!
TOSS
HEY! DON'T THROW IT!
urk

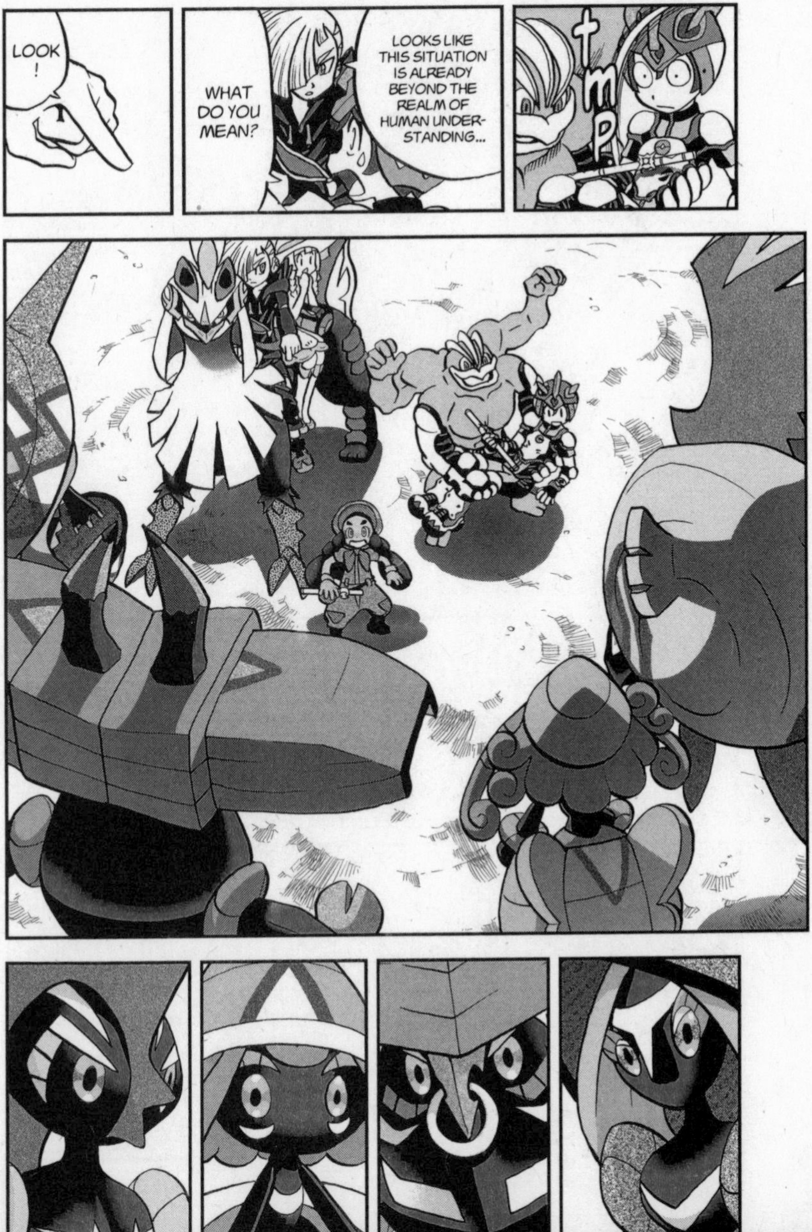
tmp
LOOKS LIKE THIS SITUATION IS ALREADY BEYOND THE REALM OF HUMAN UNDER-STANDING...
WHAT DO YOU MEAN?
LOOK !

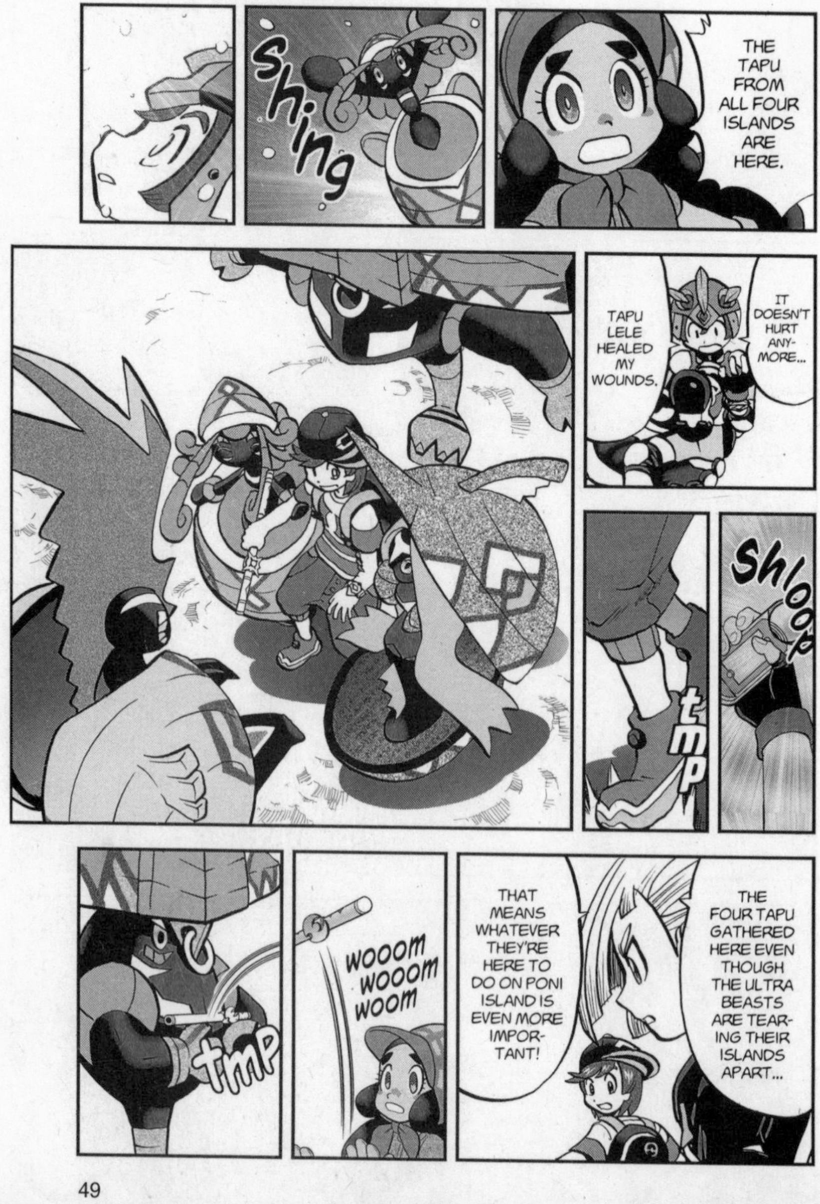
THE TAPU FROM ALL FOUR ISLANDS ARE HERE.
Shing
IT DOESN'T HURT ANY-MORE...
TAPU LELE HEALED MY WOUNDS.
Shlooop
tmp
THE FOUR TAPU GATHERED HERE EVEN THOUGH THE ULTRA BEASTS ARE TEAR-ING THEIR ISLANDS APART...
THAT MEANS WHATEVER THEY'RE HERE TO DO ON PONI ISLAND IS EVEN MORE IMPOR-TANT!
WOOOM WOOOM WOOM
tmp

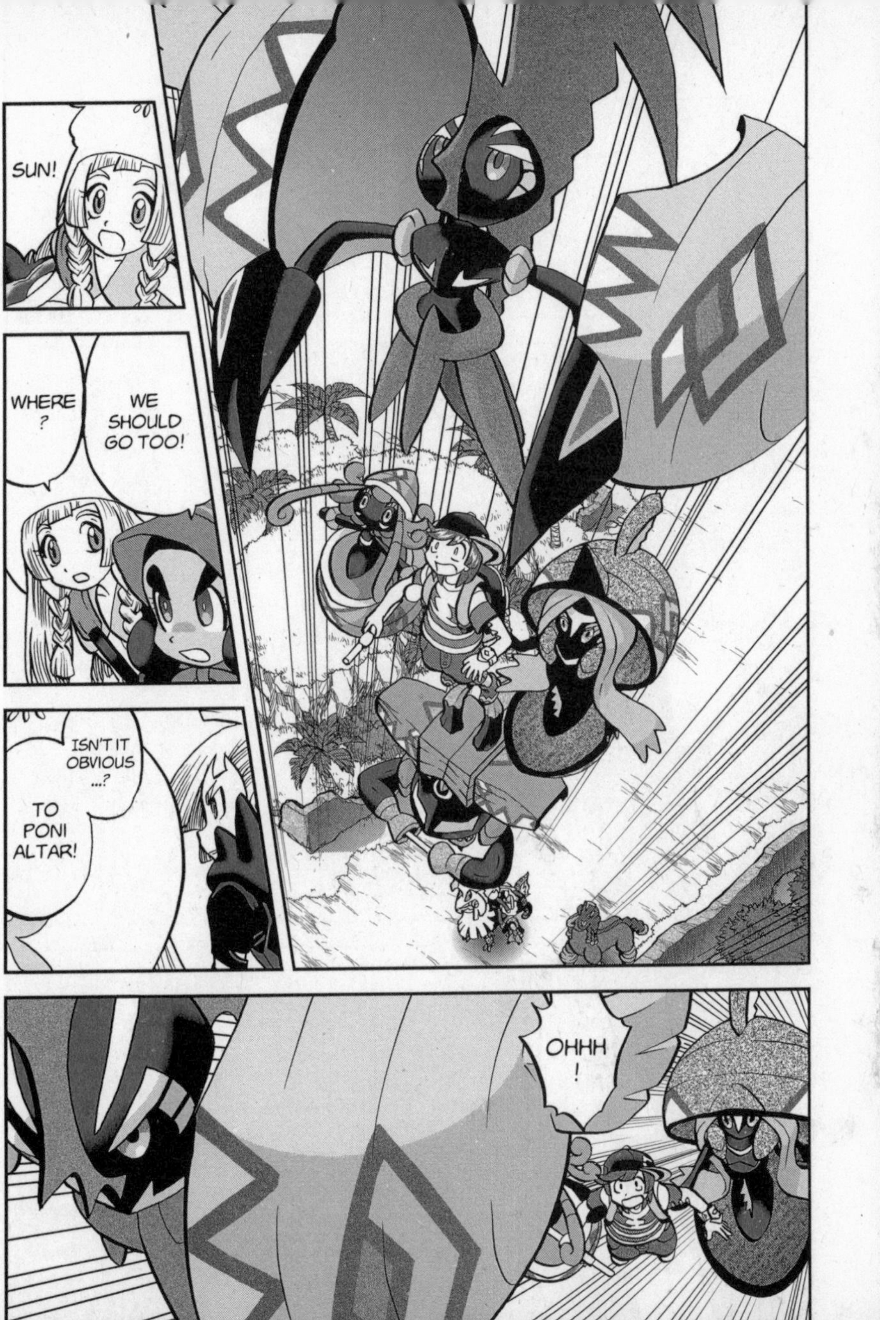
SUN!
WE SHOULD GO TOO!
WHERE?
ISN'T IT OBVIOUS...?
TO PONI ALTAR!
OHHH!

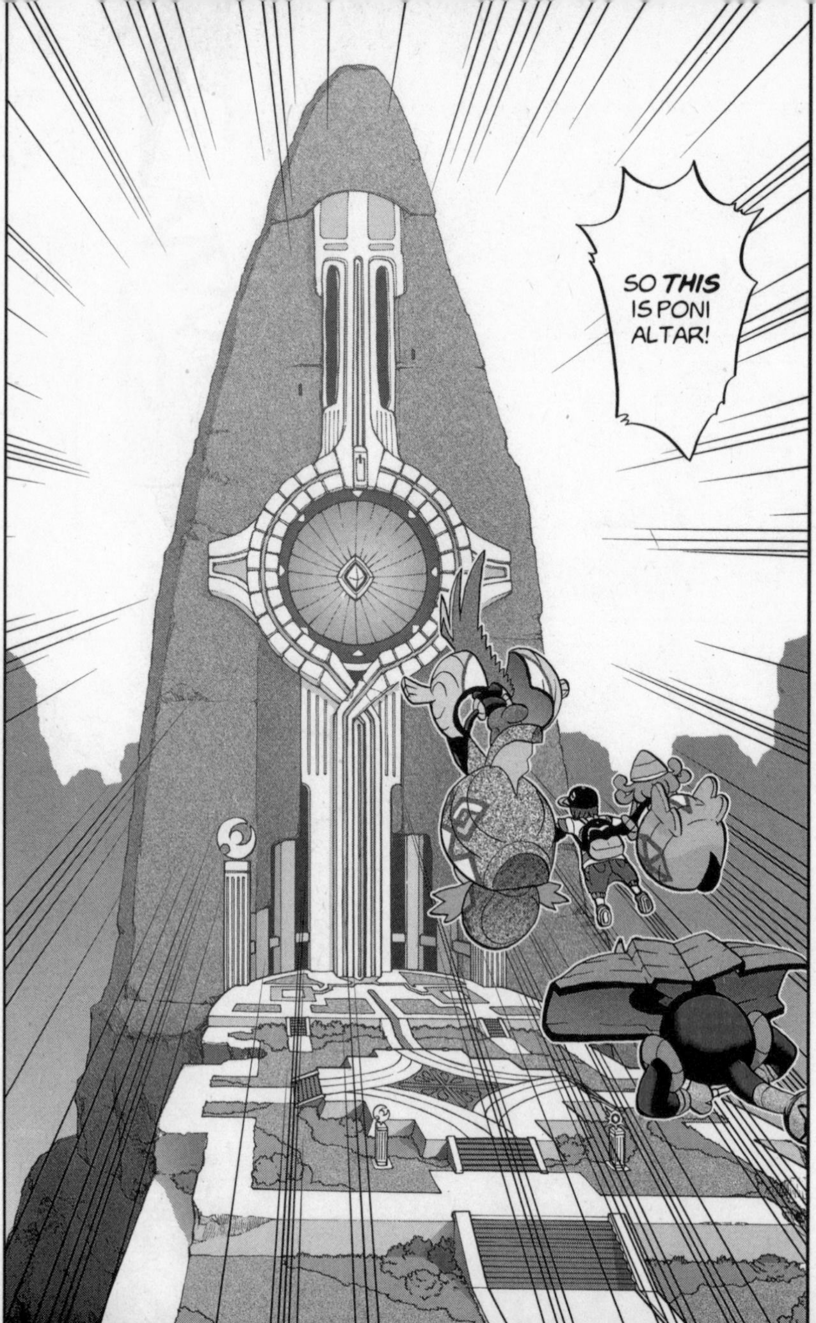
SO THIS IS PONI ALTAR!

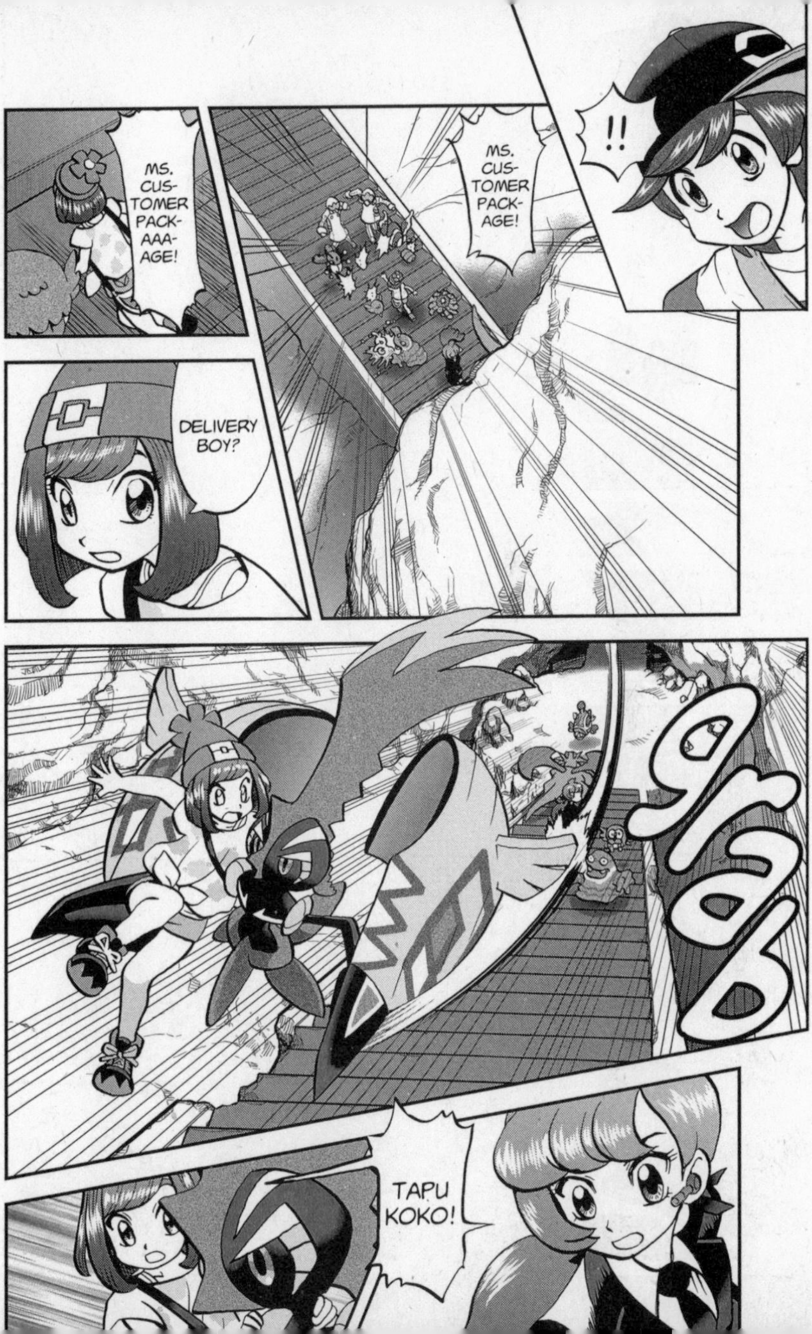
!!
MS. CUSTOMER PACKAGE!
MS. CUSTOMER PACKAAAAGE!
DELIVERY BOY?
grab
TAPU KOKO!

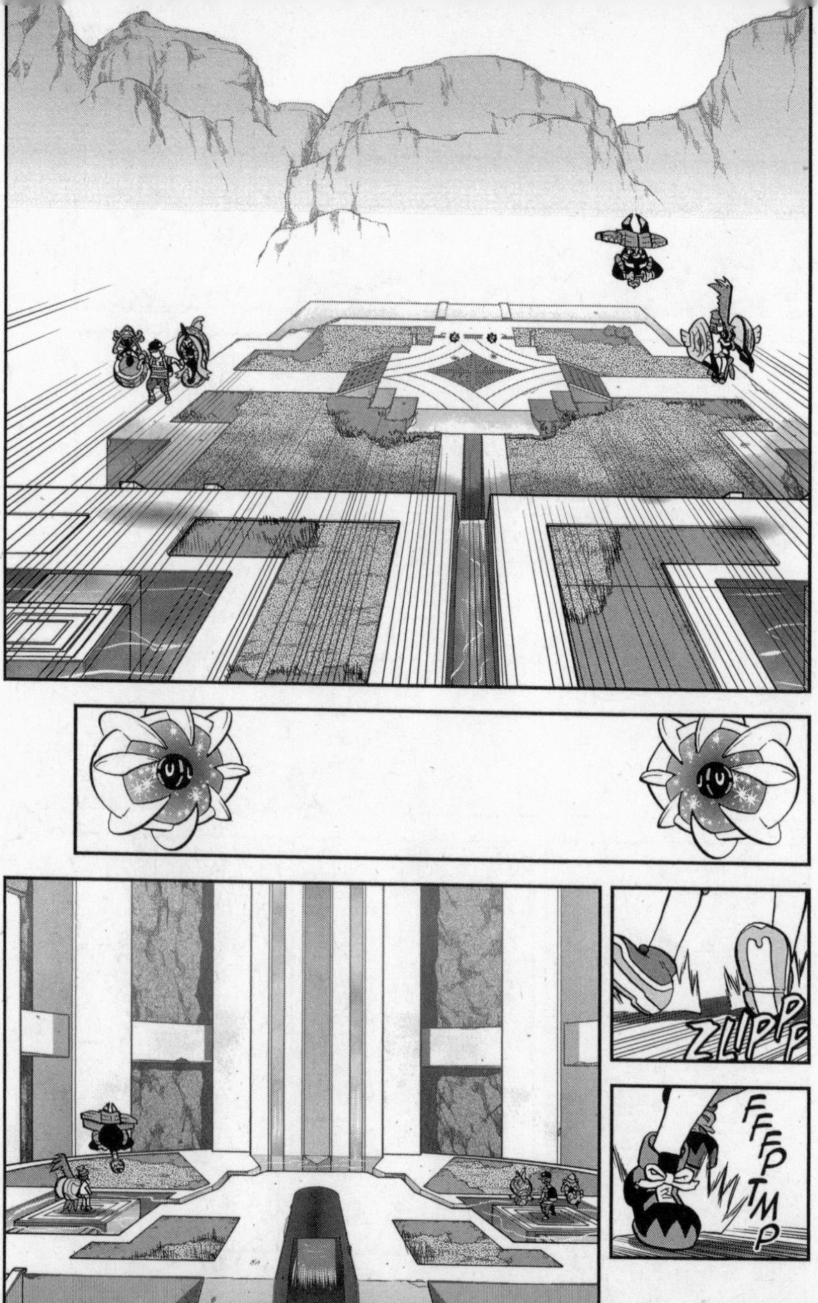
ZLIPPP
FFFPTMP

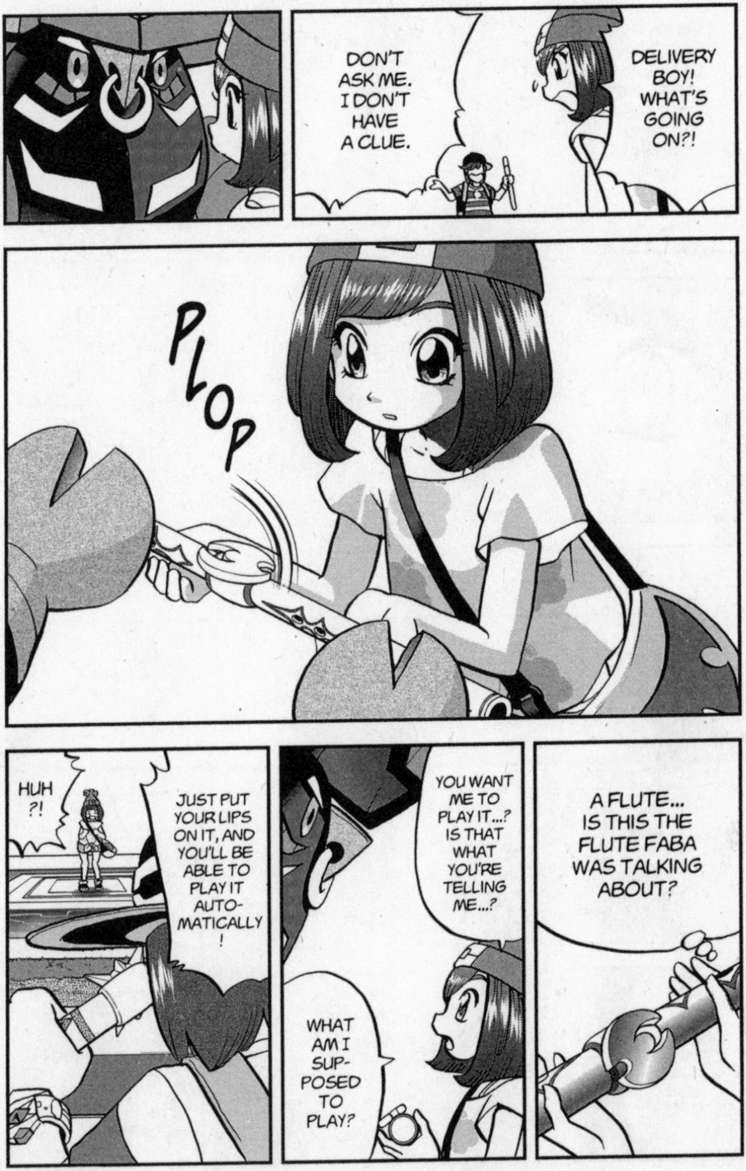
DELIVERY BOY! WHAT'S GOING ON?!
DON'T ASK ME. I DON'T HAVE A CLUE.
PLOP
A FLUTE... IS THIS THE FLUTE FABA WAS TALKING ABOUT?
YOU WANT ME TO PLAY IT...? IS THAT WHAT YOU'RE TELLING ME...?
WHAT AM I SUP-POSED TO PLAY?
JUST PUT YOUR LIPS ON IT, AND YOU'LL BE ABLE TO PLAY IT AUTO-MATICALLY!
HUH?!

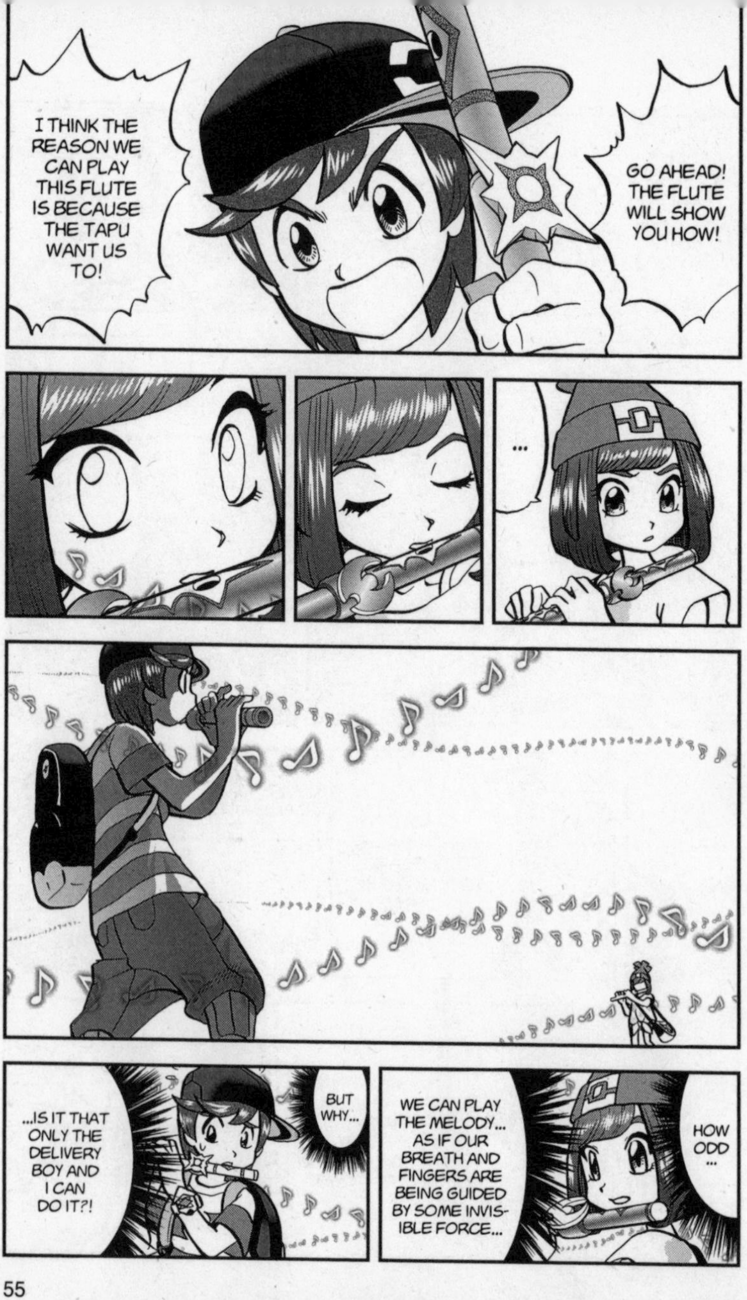
GO AHEAD! THE FLUTE WILL SHOW YOU HOW!
I THINK THE REASON WE CAN PLAY THIS FLUTE IS BECAUSE THE TAPU WANT US TO!
...
HOW ODD...
WE CAN PLAY THE MELODY... AS IF OUR BREATH AND FINGERS ARE BEING GUIDED BY SOME INVISIBLE FORCE...
BUT WHY...
...IS IT THAT ONLY THE DELIVERY BOY AND I CAN DO IT?!

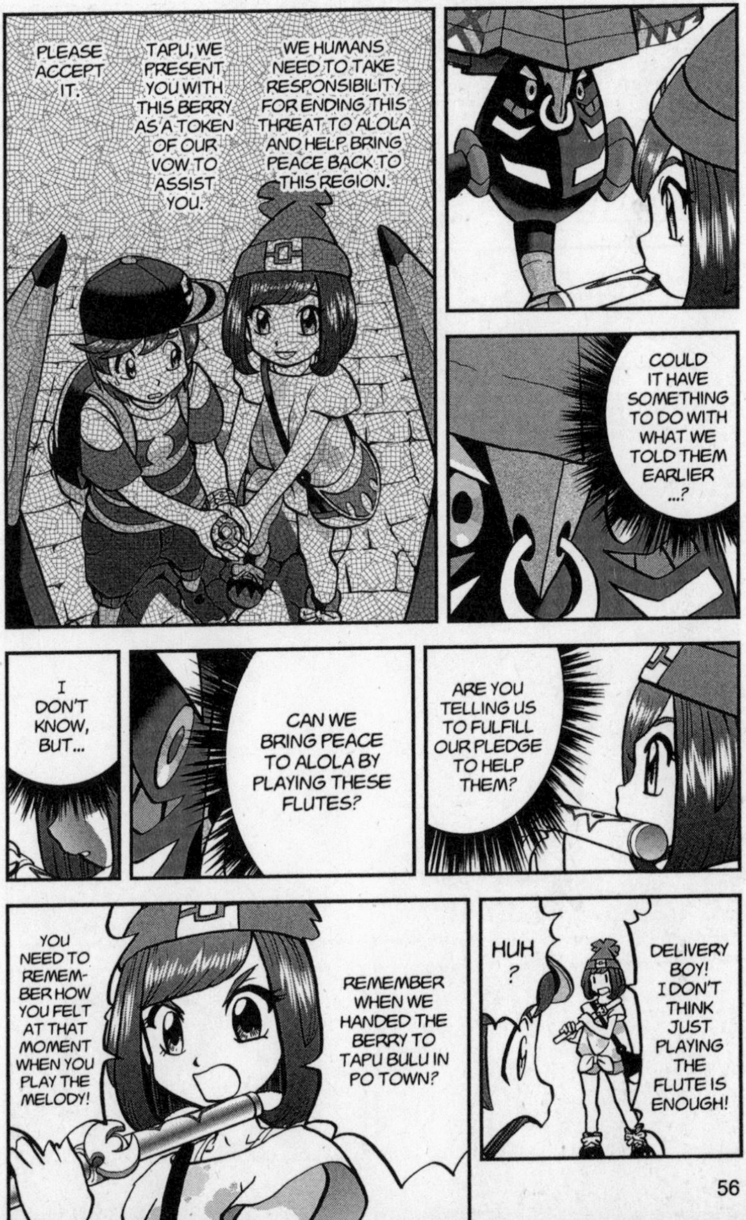
COULD IT HAVE SOMETHING TO DO WITH WHAT WE TOLD THEM EARLIER ...?
WE HUMANS NEED TO TAKE RESPONSIBILITY FOR ENDING THIS THREAT TO ALOLA AND HELP BRING PEACE BACK TO THIS REGION.
TAPU, WE PRESENT YOU WITH THIS BERRY AS A TOKEN OF OUR VOW TO ASSIST YOU.
PLEASE ACCEPT IT.
ARE YOU TELLING US TO FULFILL OUR PLEDGE TO HELP THEM?
CAN WE BRING PEACE TO ALOLA BY PLAYING THESE FLUTES?
I DON'T KNOW, BUT...
DELIVERY BOY! I DON'T THINK JUST PLAYING THE FLUTE IS ENOUGH!
HUH?
REMEMBER WHEN WE HANDED THE BERRY TO TAPU BULU IN PO TOWN?
YOU NEED TO REMEM-BER HOW YOU FELT AT THAT MOMENT WHEN YOU PLAY THE MELODY!

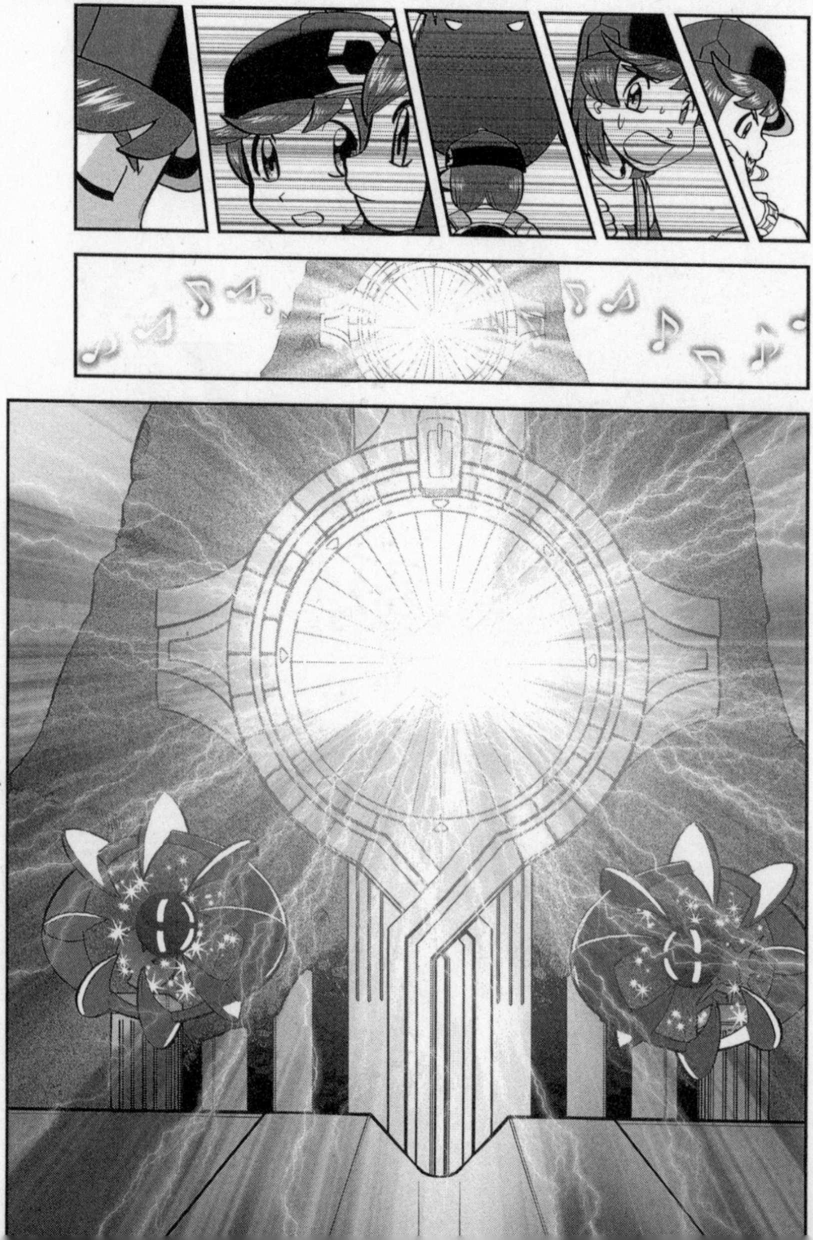

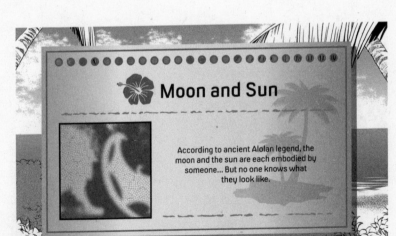

Moon and Sun

According to ancient Alolan legend, the moon and the sun are each embodied by someone... But no one knows what they look like.

Guide to Alola 21

Adventure 25 Summon the Emissaries of the Moon and the Sun

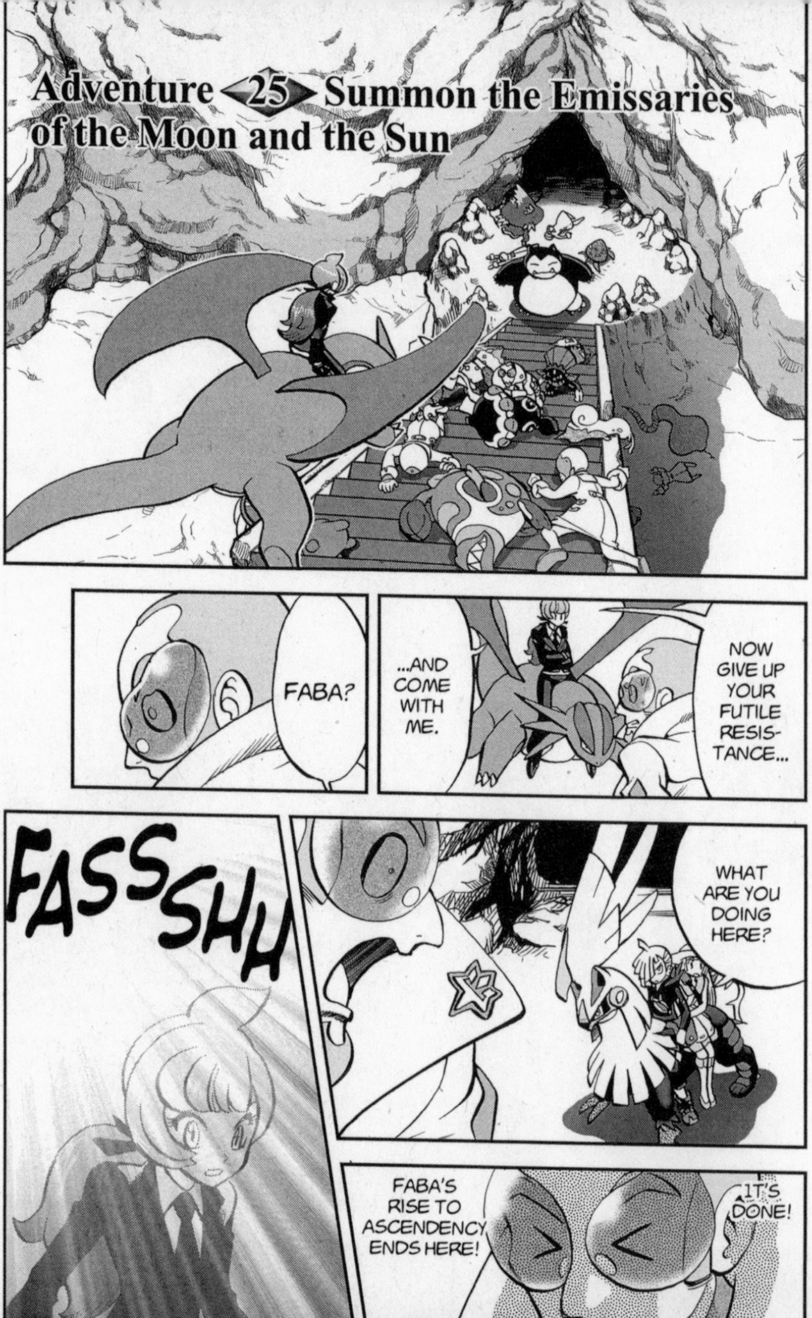
NOW GIVE UP YOUR FUTILE RESISTANCE...
...AND COME WITH ME.
FABA?
WHAT ARE YOU DOING HERE?
IT'S DONE!
FABA'S RISE TO ASCENDENCY ENDS HERE!
FASSHH

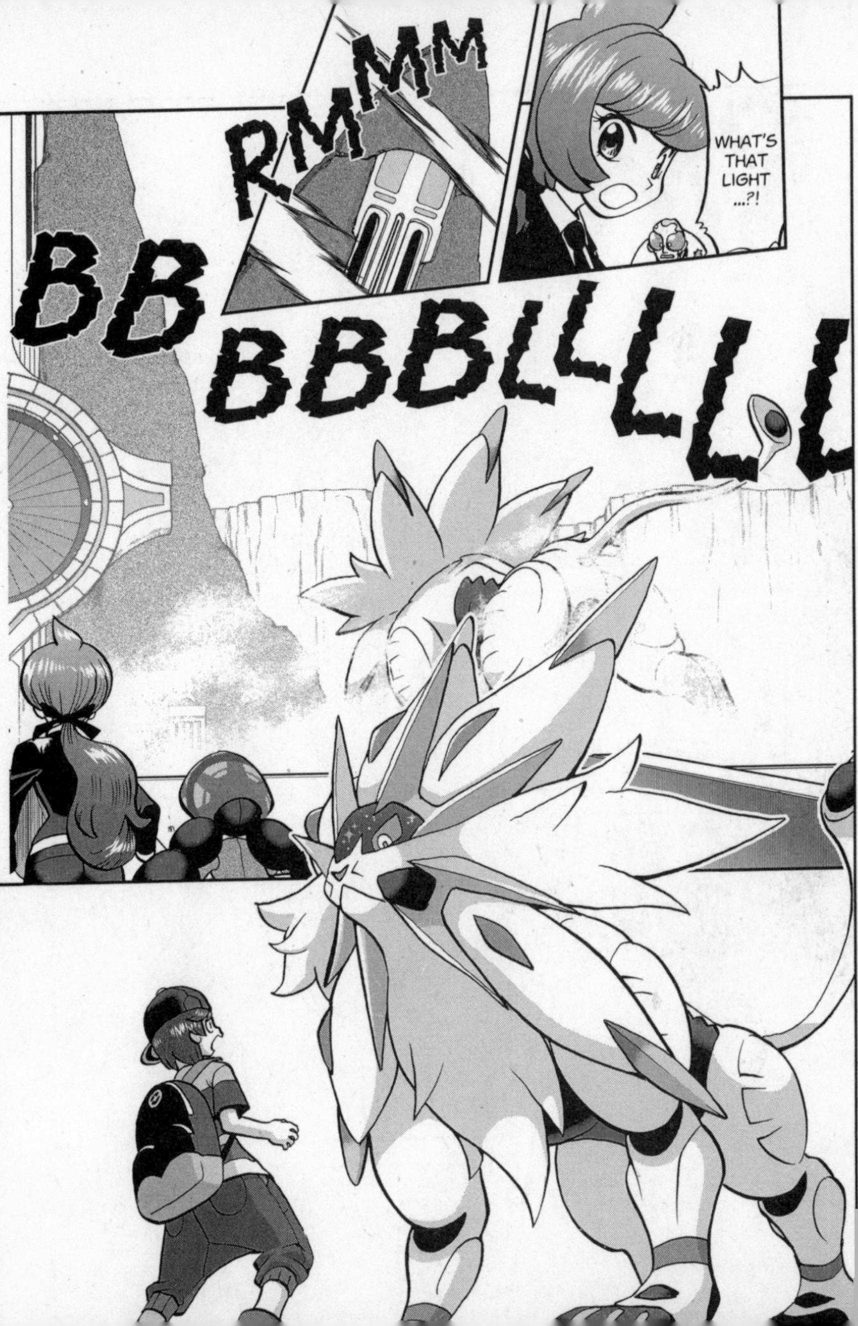
WHAT'S THAT LIGHT ...?!
RMMMM
BBBBBLLLLL

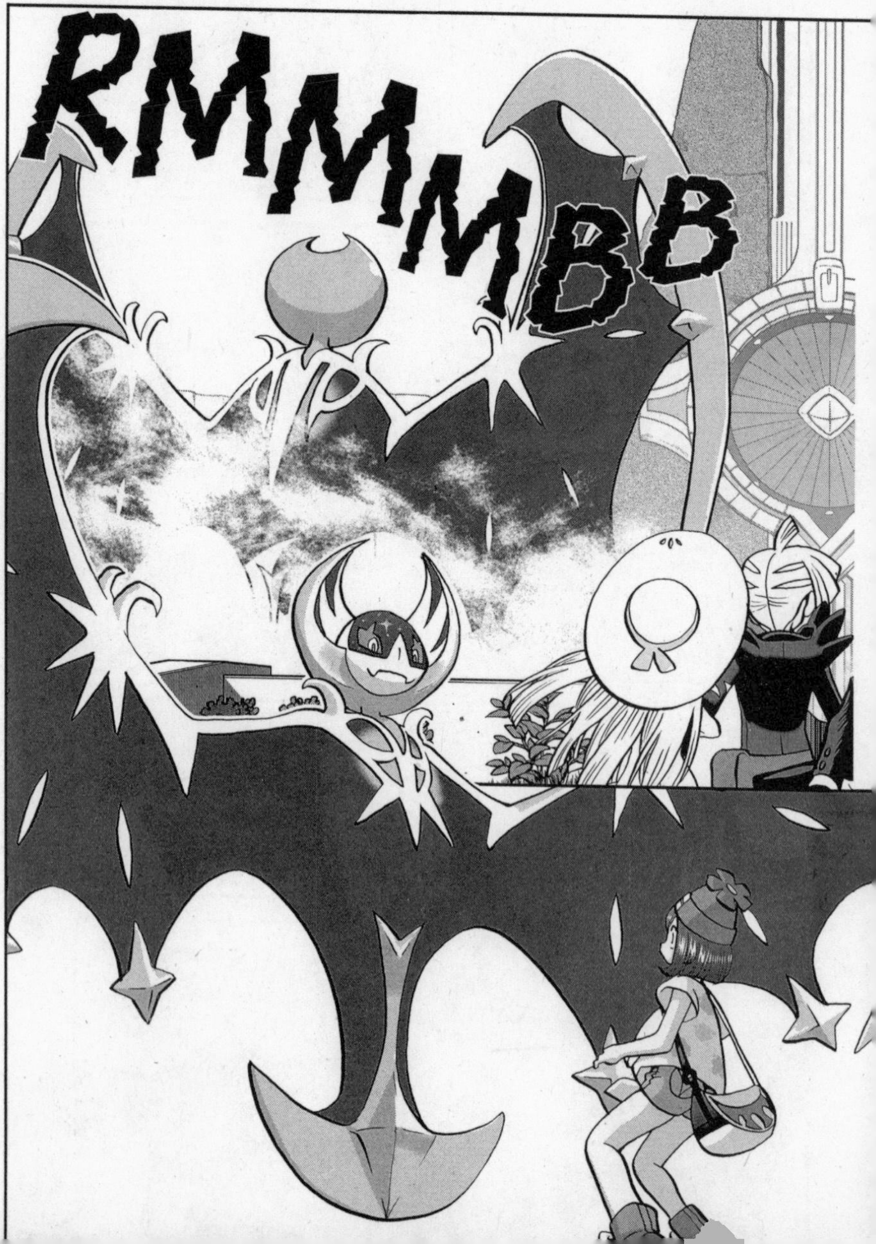
RMMMMBB

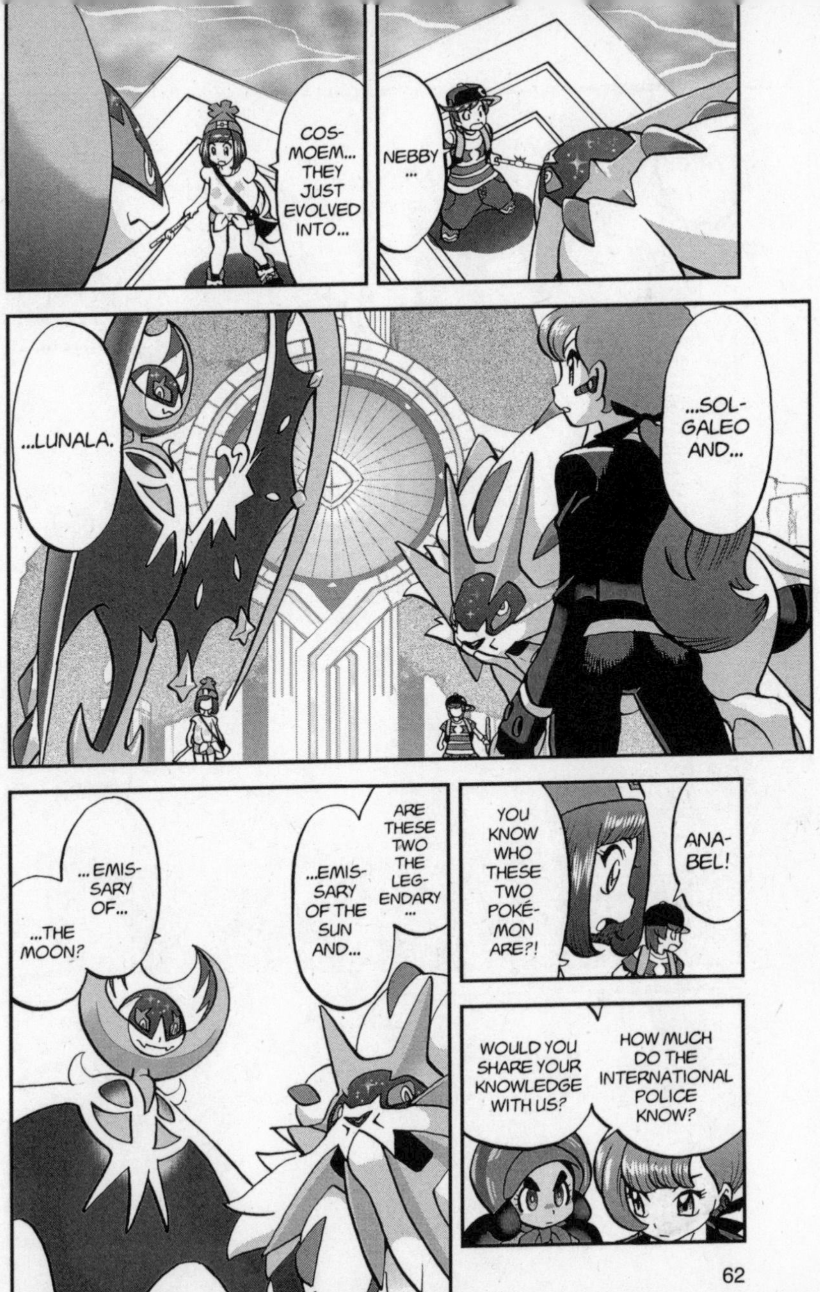
NEBBY ...
COS-MOEM... THEY JUST EVOLVED INTO...
...SOL-GALEO AND...
...LUNALA.
ANA-BEL!
YOU KNOW WHO THESE TWO POKÉ-MON ARE?!
HOW MUCH DO THE INTERNATIONAL POLICE KNOW?
WOULD YOU SHARE YOUR KNOWLEDGE WITH US?
ARE THESE TWO THE LEG-ENDARY ...
...EMIS-SARY OF THE SUN AND...
... EMIS-SARY OF...
...THE MOON?

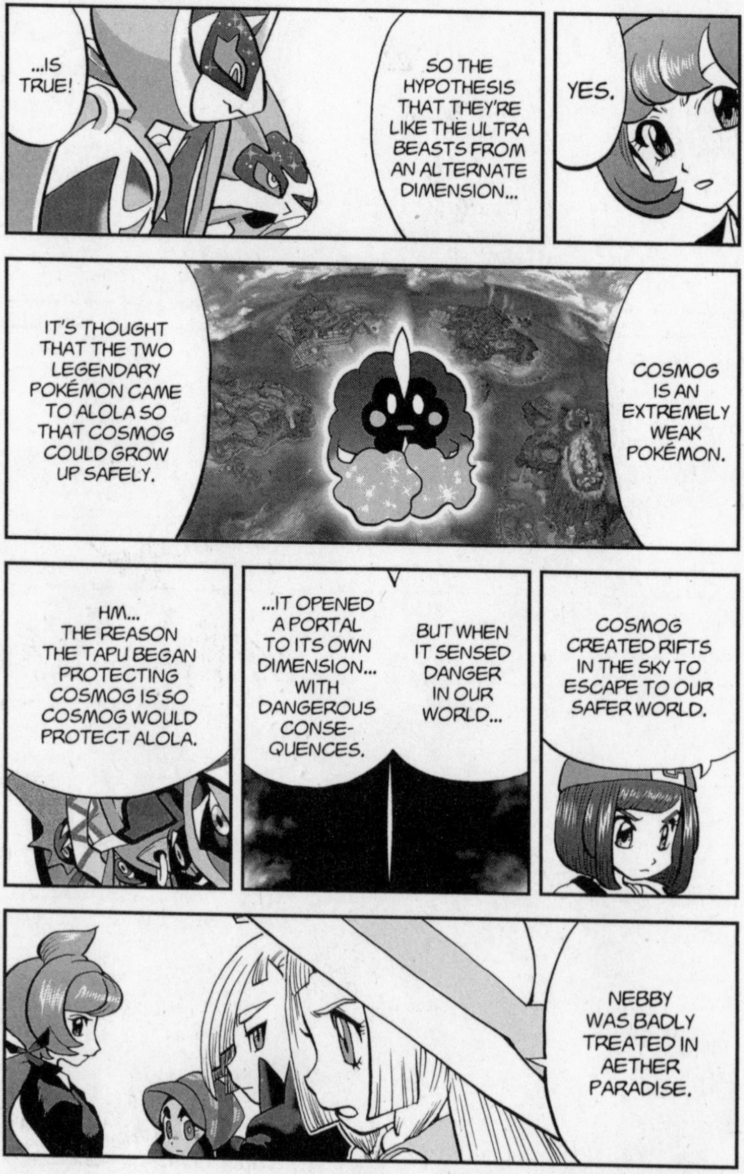
YES.
SO THE HYPOTHESIS THAT THEY'RE LIKE THE ULTRA BEASTS FROM AN ALTERNATE DIMENSION...
...IS TRUE!
COSMOG IS AN EXTREMELY WEAK POKÉMON.
IT'S THOUGHT THAT THE TWO LEGENDARY POKÉMON CAME TO ALOLA SO THAT COSMOG COULD GROW UP SAFELY.
COSMOG CREATED RIFTS IN THE SKY TO ESCAPE TO OUR SAFER WORLD.
BUT WHEN IT SENSED DANGER IN OUR WORLD...
...IT OPENED A PORTAL TO ITS OWN DIMENSION... WITH DANGEROUS CONSE-QUENCES.
HM... THE REASON THE TAPU BEGAN PROTECTING COSMOG IS SO COSMOG WOULD PROTECT ALOLA.
NEBBY WAS BADLY TREATED IN AETHER PARADISE.

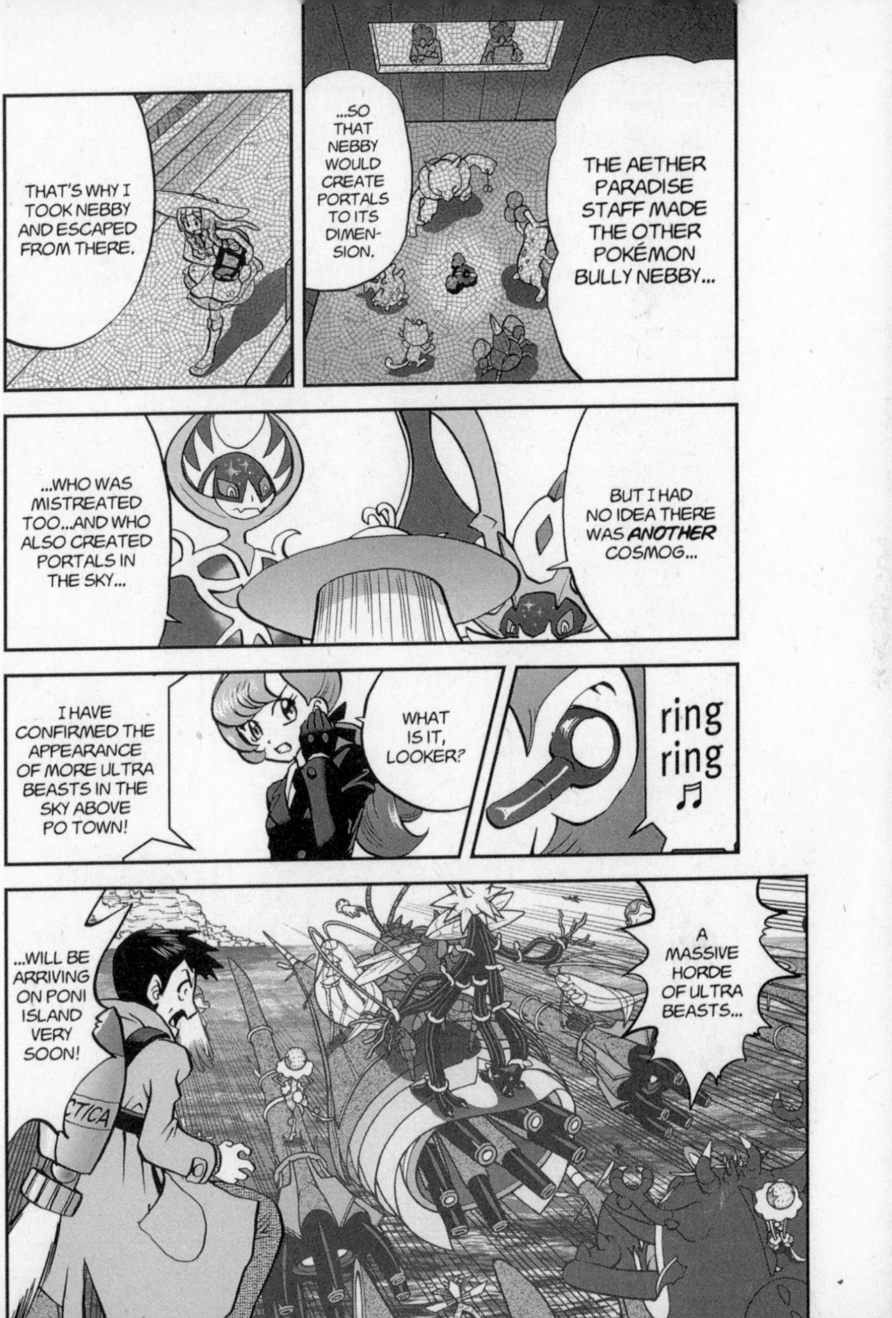
THE AETHER PARADISE STAFF MADE THE OTHER POKÉMON BULLY NEBBY...
...SO THAT NEBBY WOULD CREATE PORTALS TO ITS DIMENSION.
THAT'S WHY I TOOK NEBBY AND ESCAPED FROM THERE.
BUT I HAD NO IDEA THERE WAS **ANOTHER** COSMOG...
...WHO WAS MISTREATED TOO...AND WHO ALSO CREATED PORTALS IN THE SKY...
ring ring ♫
WHAT IS IT, LOOKER?
I HAVE CONFIRMED THE APPEARANCE OF MORE ULTRA BEASTS IN THE SKY ABOVE PO TOWN!
A MASSIVE HORDE OF ULTRA BEASTS...
...WILL BE ARRIVING ON PONI ISLAND VERY SOON!

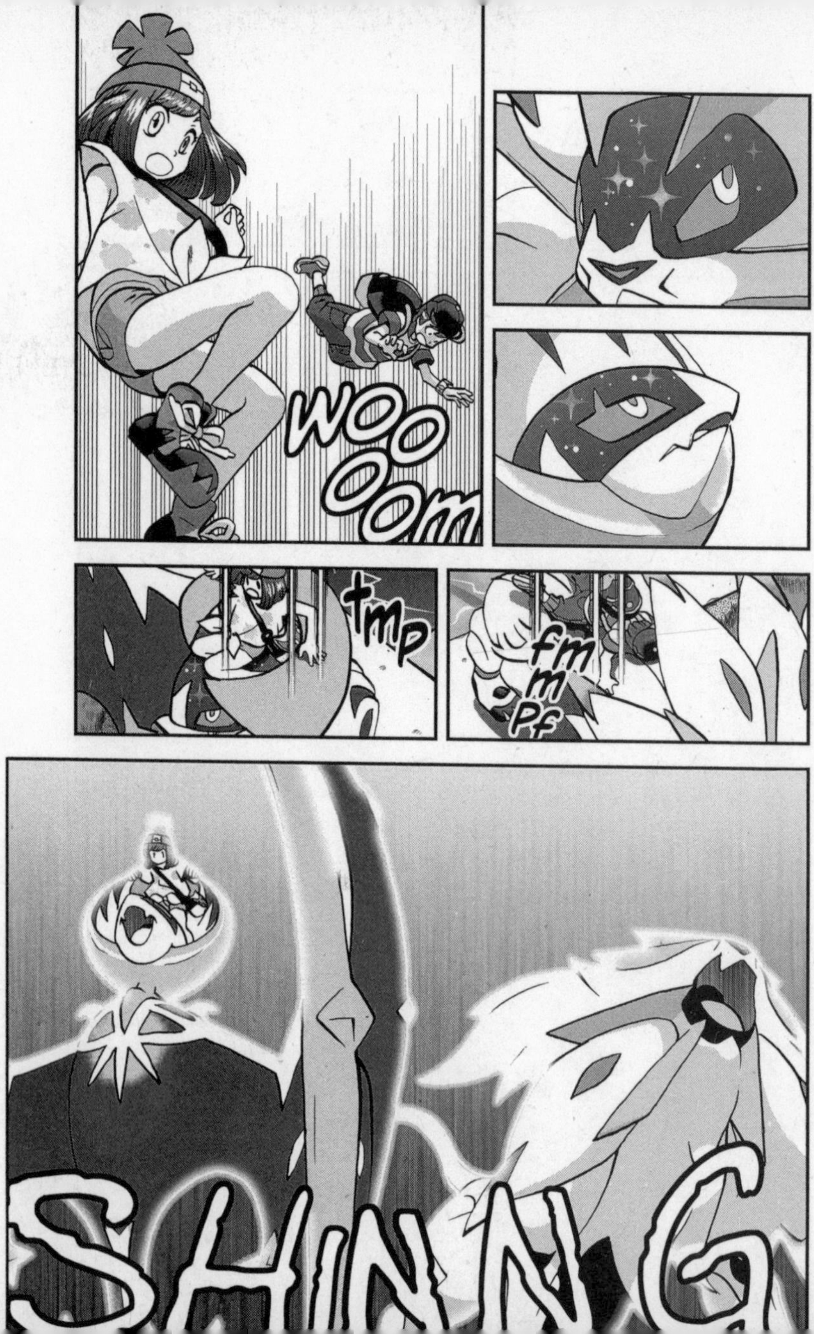
WOOOOOM
fmmPf
tmp
SHINNG

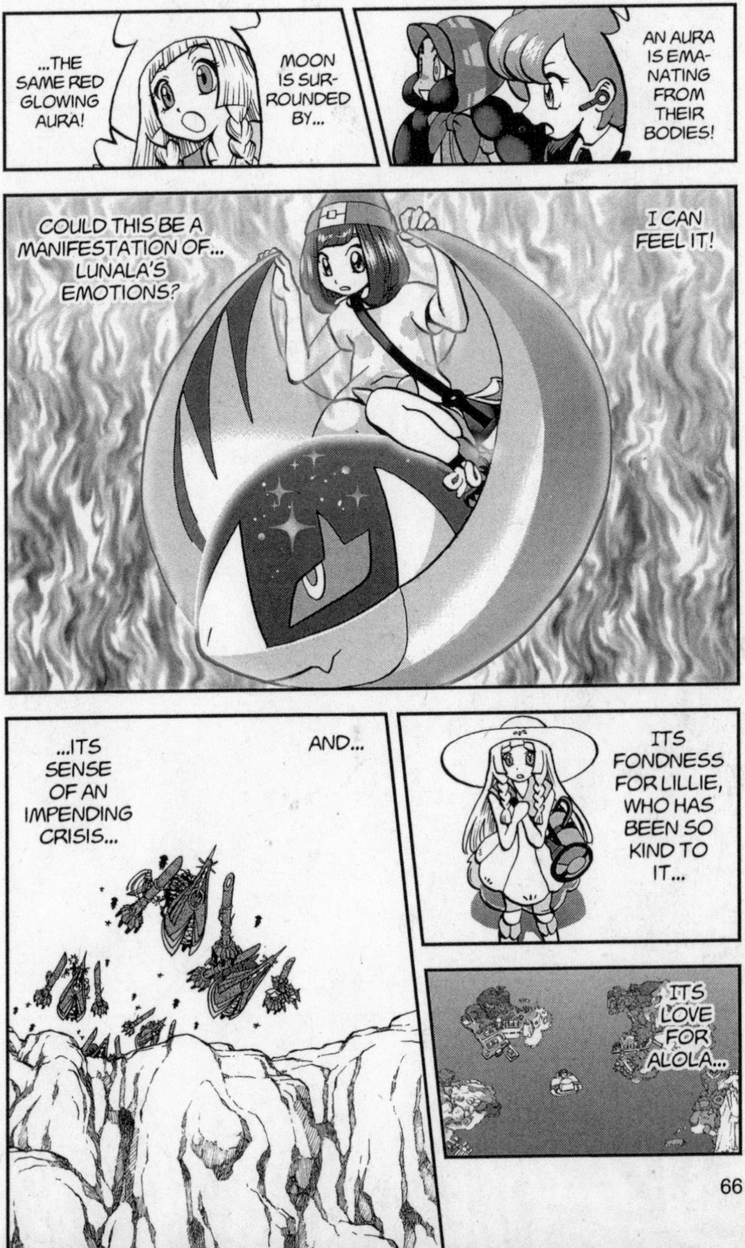
AN AURA IS EMA-NATING FROM THEIR BODIES!
MOON IS SUR-ROUNDED BY...
...THE SAME RED GLOWING AURA!
I CAN FEEL IT!
COULD THIS BE A MANIFESTATION OF... LUNALA'S EMOTIONS?
ITS FONDNESS FOR LILLIE, WHO HAS BEEN SO KIND TO IT...
ITS LOVE FOR ALOLA...
AND...
...ITS SENSE OF AN IMPENDING CRISIS...

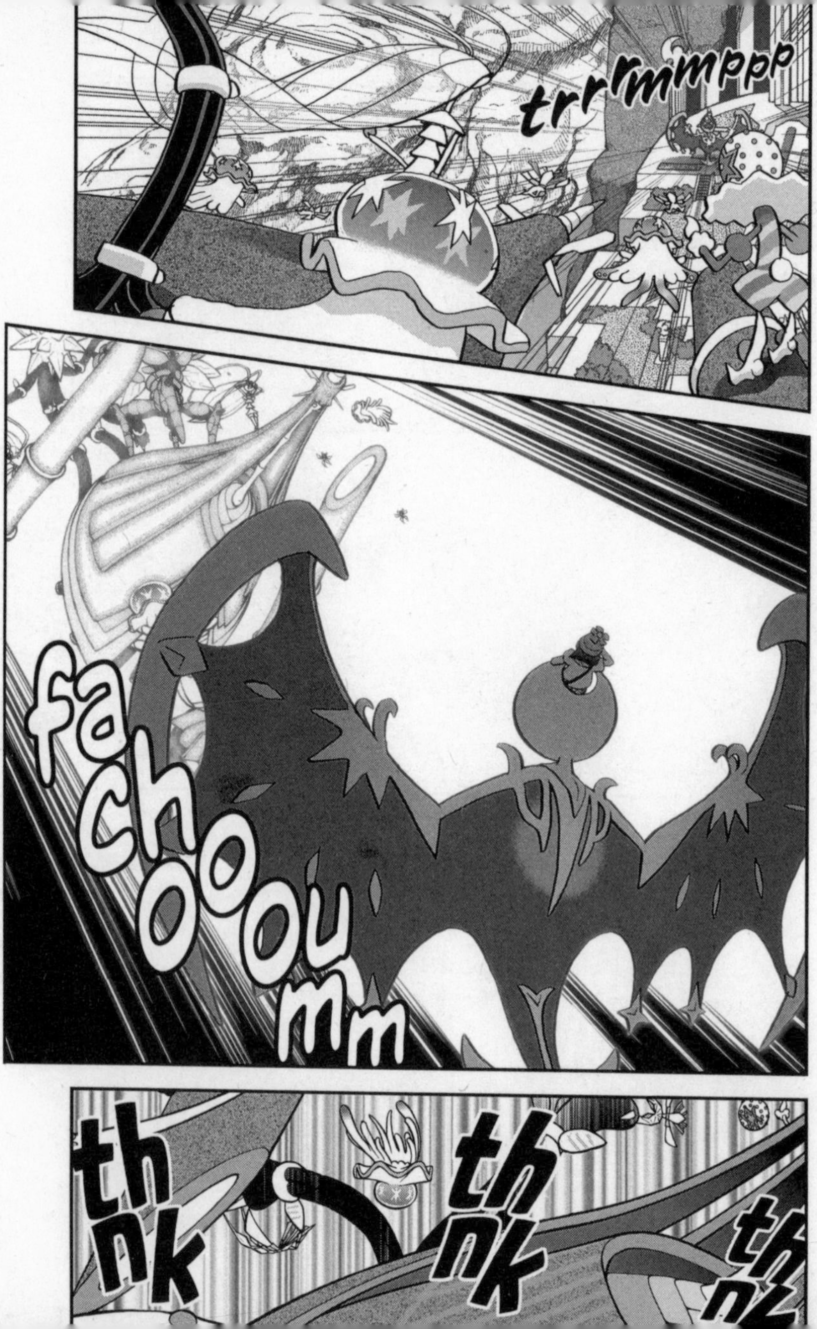
trrrmmppp
fachooooumm
thnk
thnk
thnk

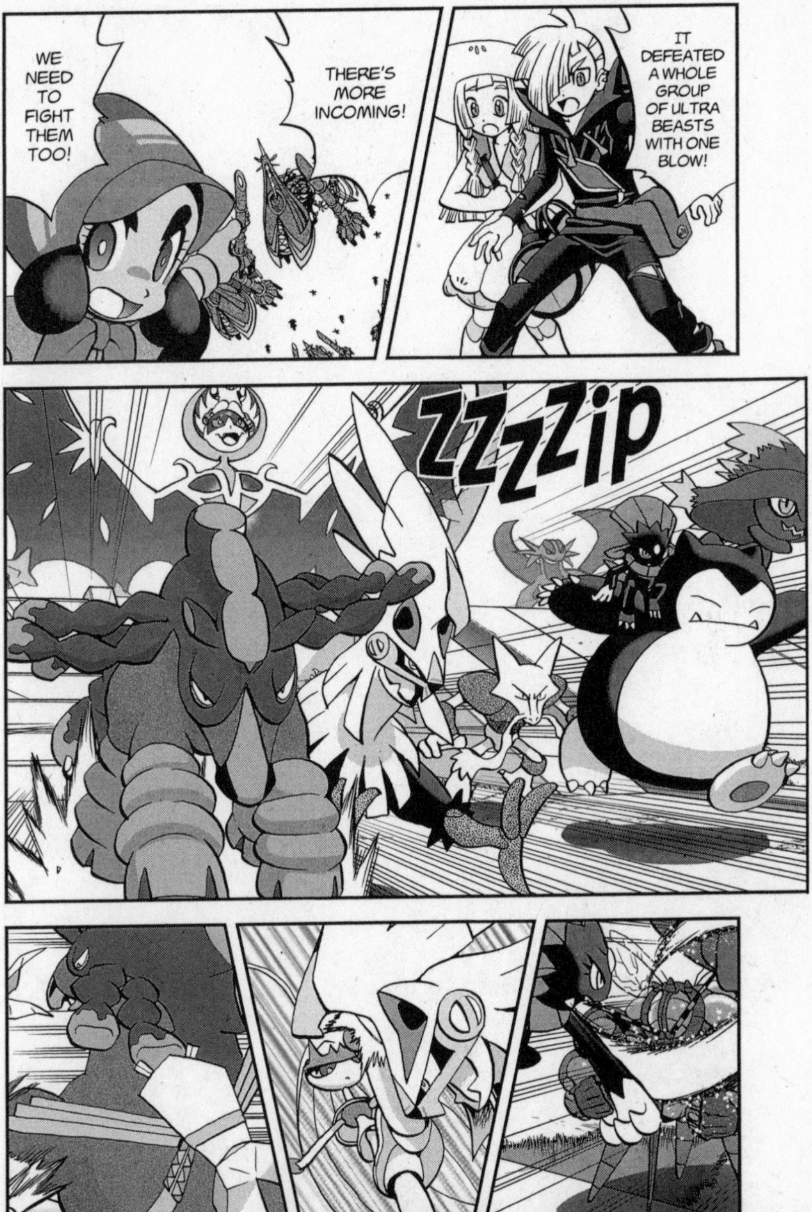
IT DEFEATED A WHOLE GROUP OF ULTRA BEASTS WITH ONE BLOW!
THERE'S MORE INCOMING!
WE NEED TO FIGHT THEM TOO!
ZZZZIP

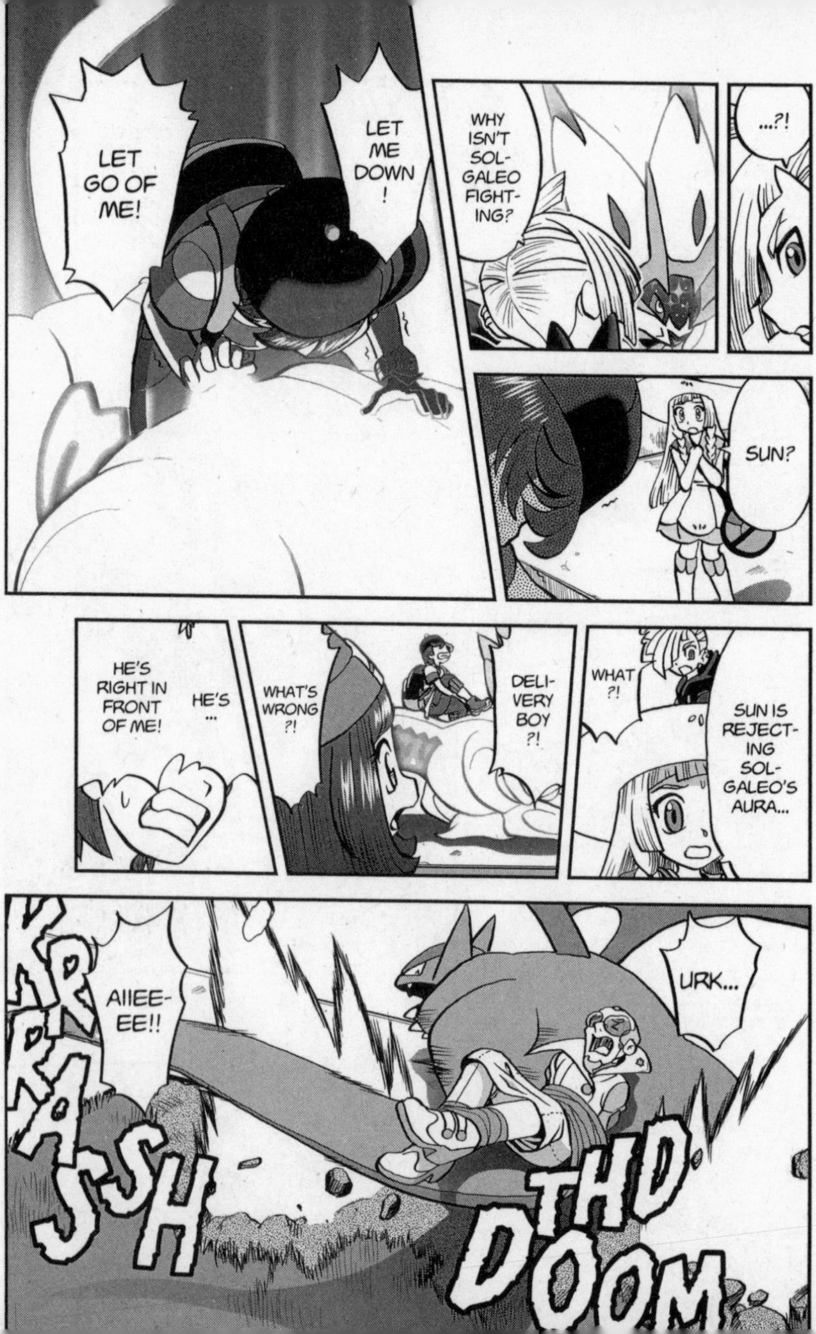
...?!
WHY ISN'T SOL-GALEO FIGHT-ING?
SUN?
LET ME DOWN!
LET GO OF ME!
SUN IS REJECT-ING SOL-GALEO'S AURA...
WHAT?!
DELI-VERY BOY?!
WHAT'S WRONG?!
HE'S...
HE'S RIGHT IN FRONT OF ME!
URK...
AIIEE-EE!!
THD DOOM
KRASH

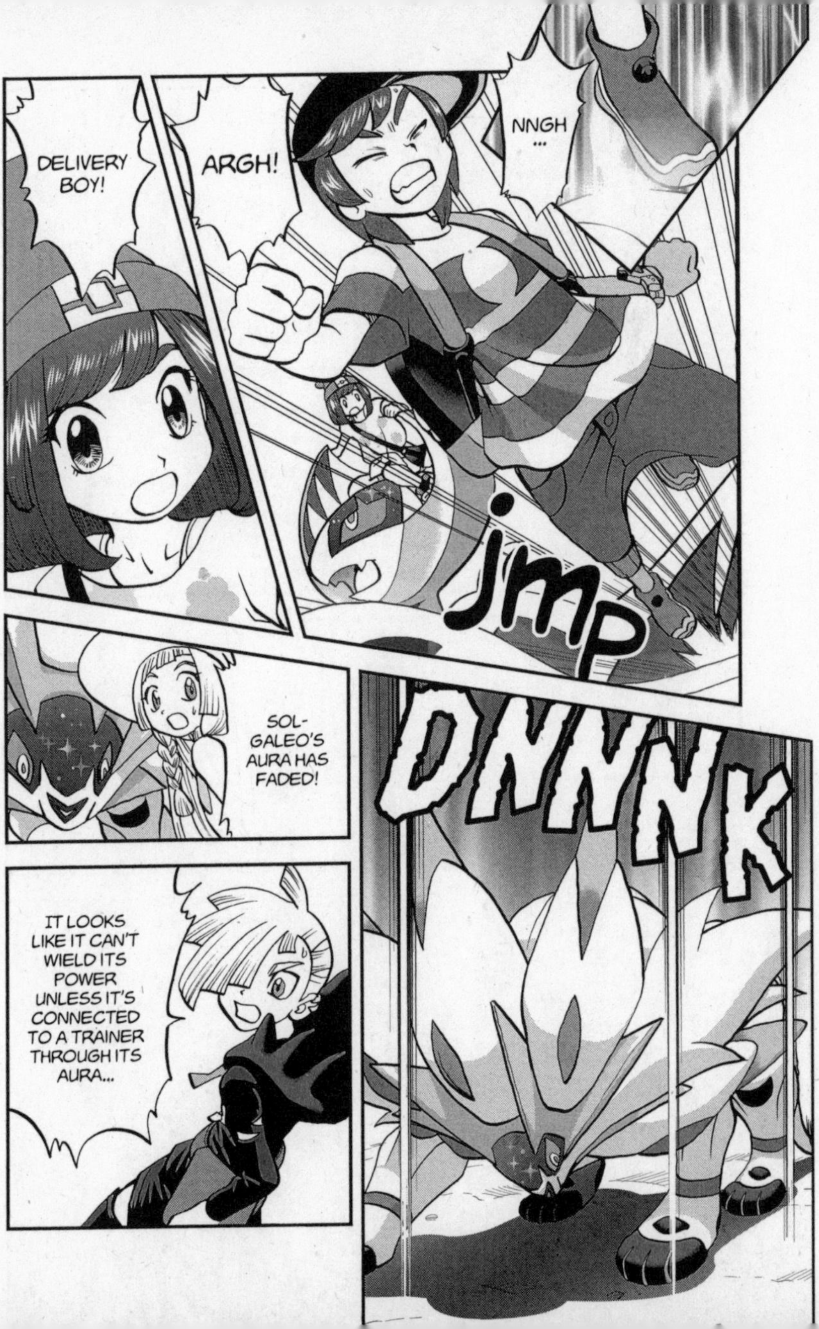
NNGH...
ARGH!
jmp
DELIVERY BOY!
DNNNK
SOL-GALEO'S AURA HAS FADED!
IT LOOKS LIKE IT CAN'T WIELD ITS POWER UNLESS IT'S CONNECTED TO A TRAINER THROUGH ITS AURA...

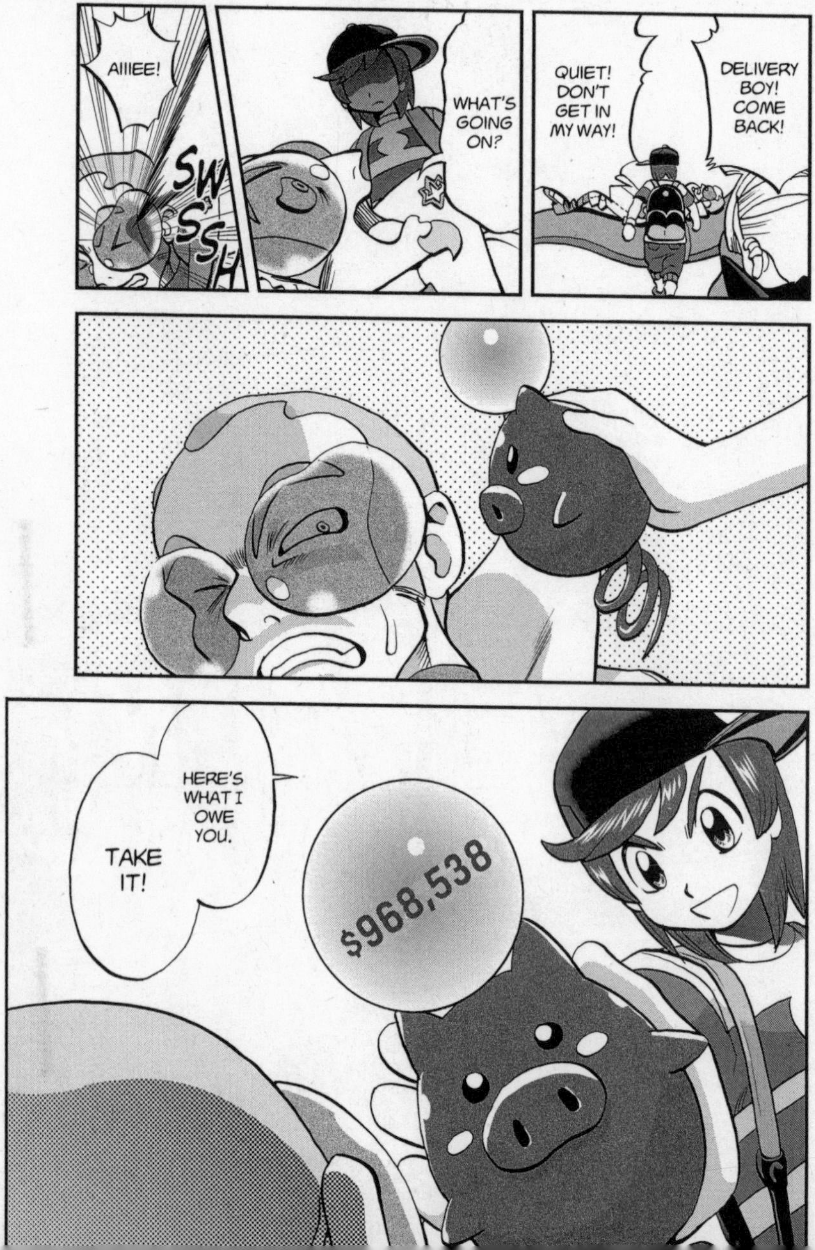
DELIVERY BOY! COME BACK!
QUIET! DON'T GET IN MY WAY!
WHAT'S GOING ON?
AIIIEE!
SWSSH
HERE'S WHAT I OWE YOU.
TAKE IT!
$968,538

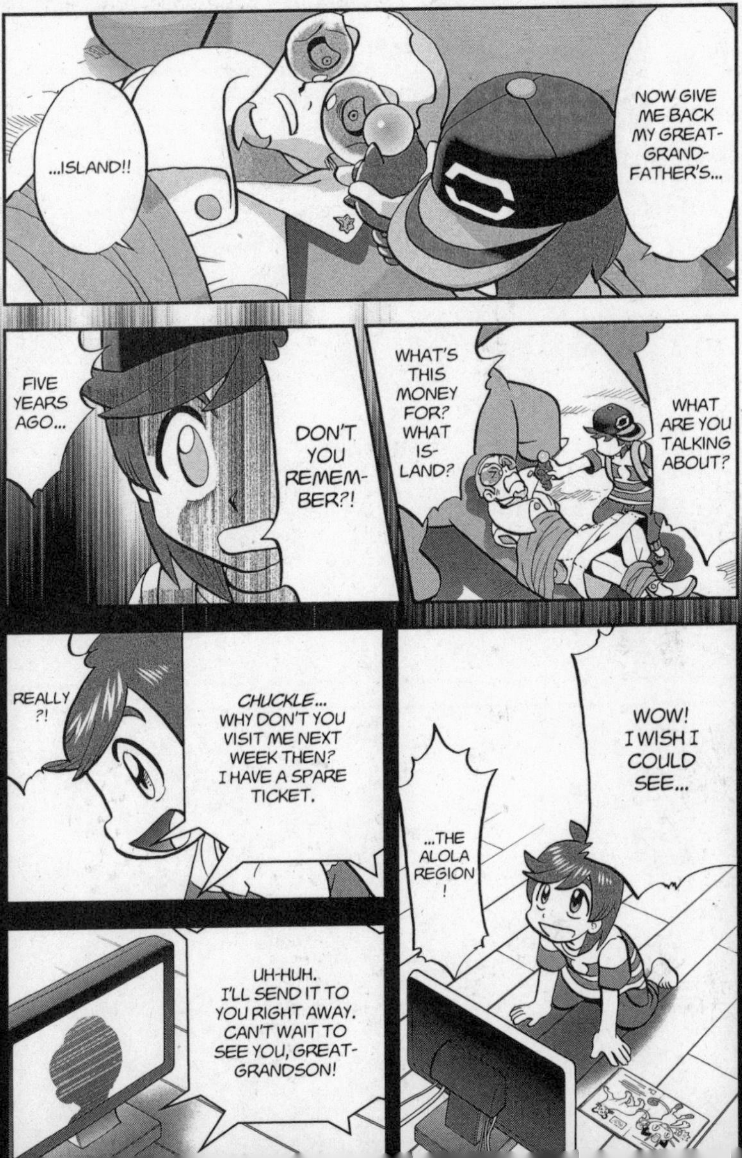
NOW GIVE ME BACK MY GREAT-GRANDFATHER'S...
...ISLAND!!
WHAT ARE YOU TALKING ABOUT?
WHAT'S THIS MONEY FOR? WHAT IS-LAND?
DON'T YOU REMEMBER?!
FIVE YEARS AGO...
WOW! I WISH I COULD SEE...
...THE ALOLA REGION!
CHUCKLE... WHY DON'T YOU VISIT ME NEXT WEEK THEN? I HAVE A SPARE TICKET.
REALLY?!
UH-HUH. I'LL SEND IT TO YOU RIGHT AWAY. CAN'T WAIT TO SEE YOU, GREAT-GRANDSON!

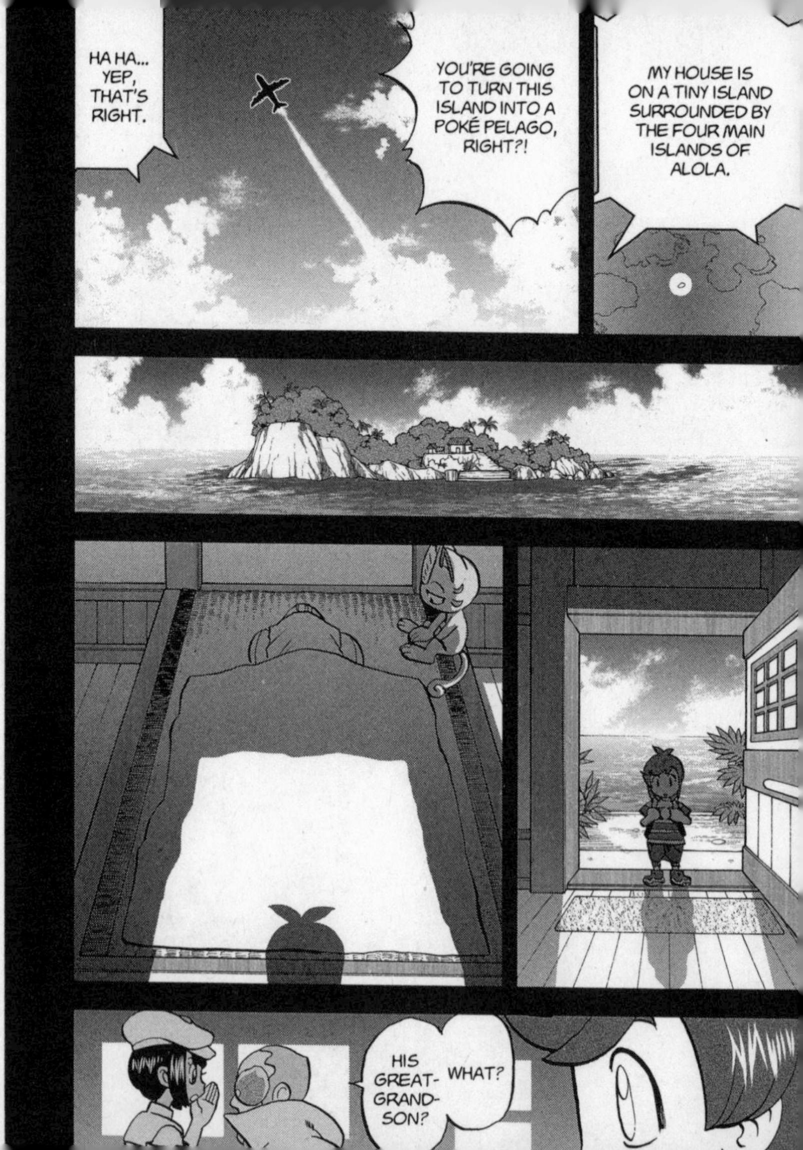
MY HOUSE IS ON A TINY ISLAND SURROUNDED BY THE FOUR MAIN ISLANDS OF ALOLA.
YOU'RE GOING TO TURN THIS ISLAND INTO A POKÉ PELAGO, RIGHT?!
HA HA... YEP, THAT'S RIGHT.
WHAT?
HIS GREAT-GRANDSON?

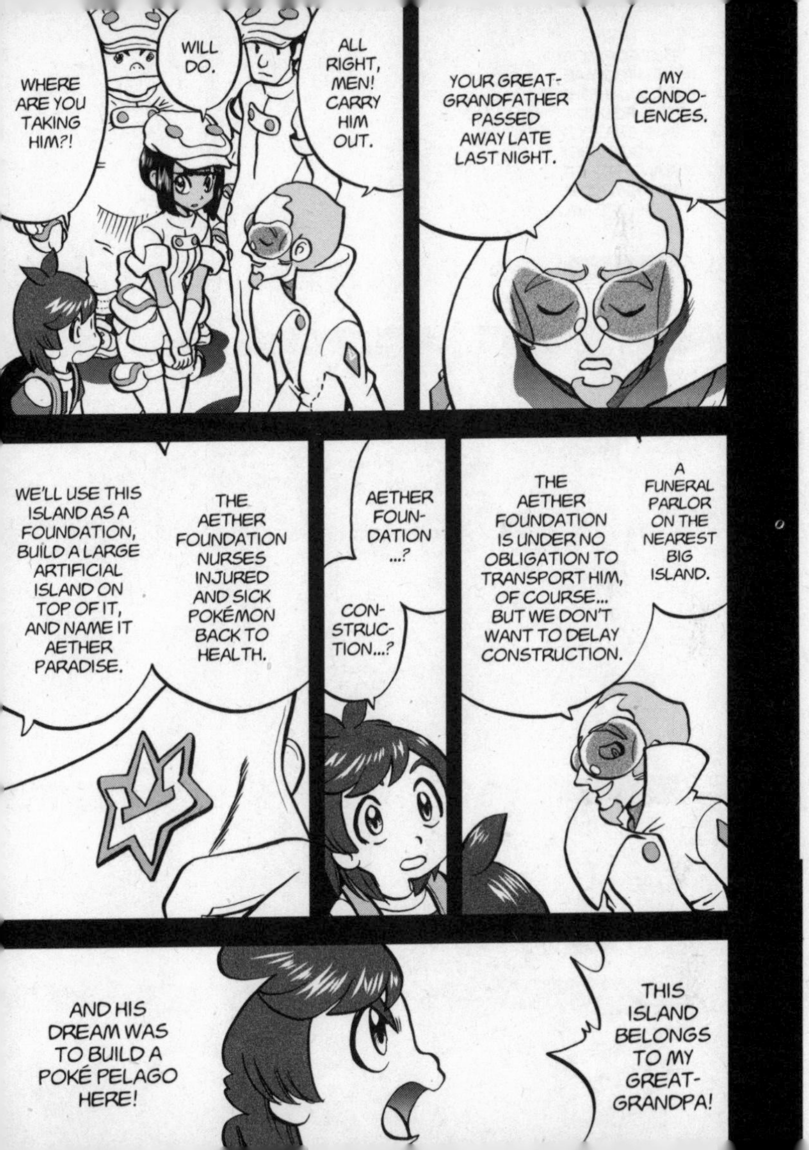
MY CONDOLENCES.
YOUR GREAT-GRANDFATHER PASSED AWAY LATE LAST NIGHT.
ALL RIGHT, MEN! CARRY HIM OUT.
WILL DO.
WHERE ARE YOU TAKING HIM?!
A FUNERAL PARLOR ON THE NEAREST BIG ISLAND.
THE AETHER FOUNDATION IS UNDER NO OBLIGATION TO TRANSPORT HIM, OF COURSE... BUT WE DON'T WANT TO DELAY CONSTRUCTION.
AETHER FOUNDATION...?
CONSTRUCTION...?
THE AETHER FOUNDATION NURSES INJURED AND SICK POKÉMON BACK TO HEALTH.
WE'LL USE THIS ISLAND AS A FOUNDATION, BUILD A LARGE ARTIFICIAL ISLAND ON TOP OF IT, AND NAME IT AETHER PARADISE.
THIS ISLAND BELONGS TO MY GREAT-GRANDPA!
AND HIS DREAM WAS TO BUILD A POKÉ PELAGO HERE!

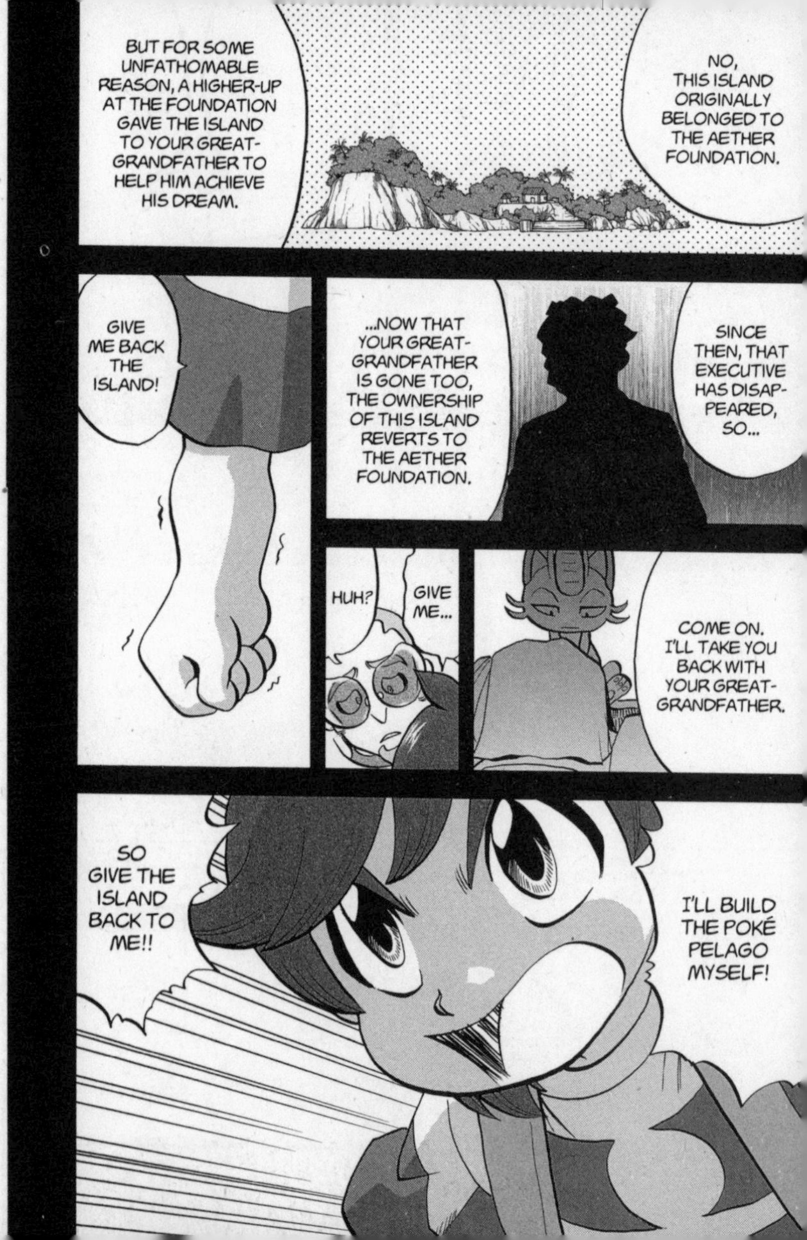
NO, THIS ISLAND ORIGINALLY BELONGED TO THE AETHER FOUNDATION.
BUT FOR SOME UNFATHOMABLE REASON, A HIGHER-UP AT THE FOUNDATION GAVE THE ISLAND TO YOUR GREAT-GRANDFATHER TO HELP HIM ACHIEVE HIS DREAM.
SINCE THEN, THAT EXECUTIVE HAS DISAP-PEARED, SO...
...NOW THAT YOUR GREAT-GRANDFATHER IS GONE TOO, THE OWNERSHIP OF THIS ISLAND REVERTS TO THE AETHER FOUNDATION.
COME ON. I'LL TAKE YOU BACK WITH YOUR GREAT-GRANDFATHER.
GIVE ME...
HUH?
GIVE ME BACK THE ISLAND!
I'LL BUILD THE POKÉ PELAGO MYSELF!
SO GIVE THE ISLAND BACK TO ME!!

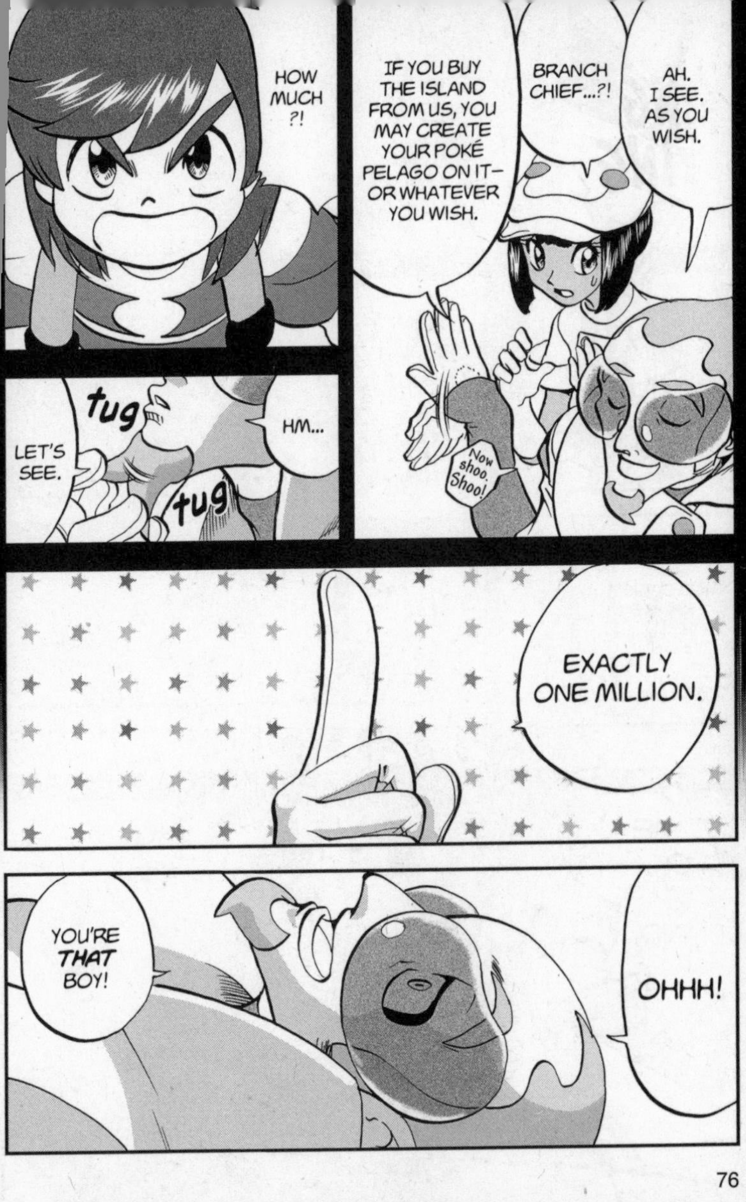
AH. I SEE. AS YOU WISH.
BRANCH CHIEF...?!
IF YOU BUY THE ISLAND FROM US, YOU MAY CREATE YOUR POKÉ PELAGO ON IT—OR WHATEVER YOU WISH.
Now shoo. Shoo!
HOW MUCH ?!
HM...
tug
LET'S SEE.
tug
EXACTLY ONE MILLION.
OHHH!
YOU'RE *THAT* BOY!

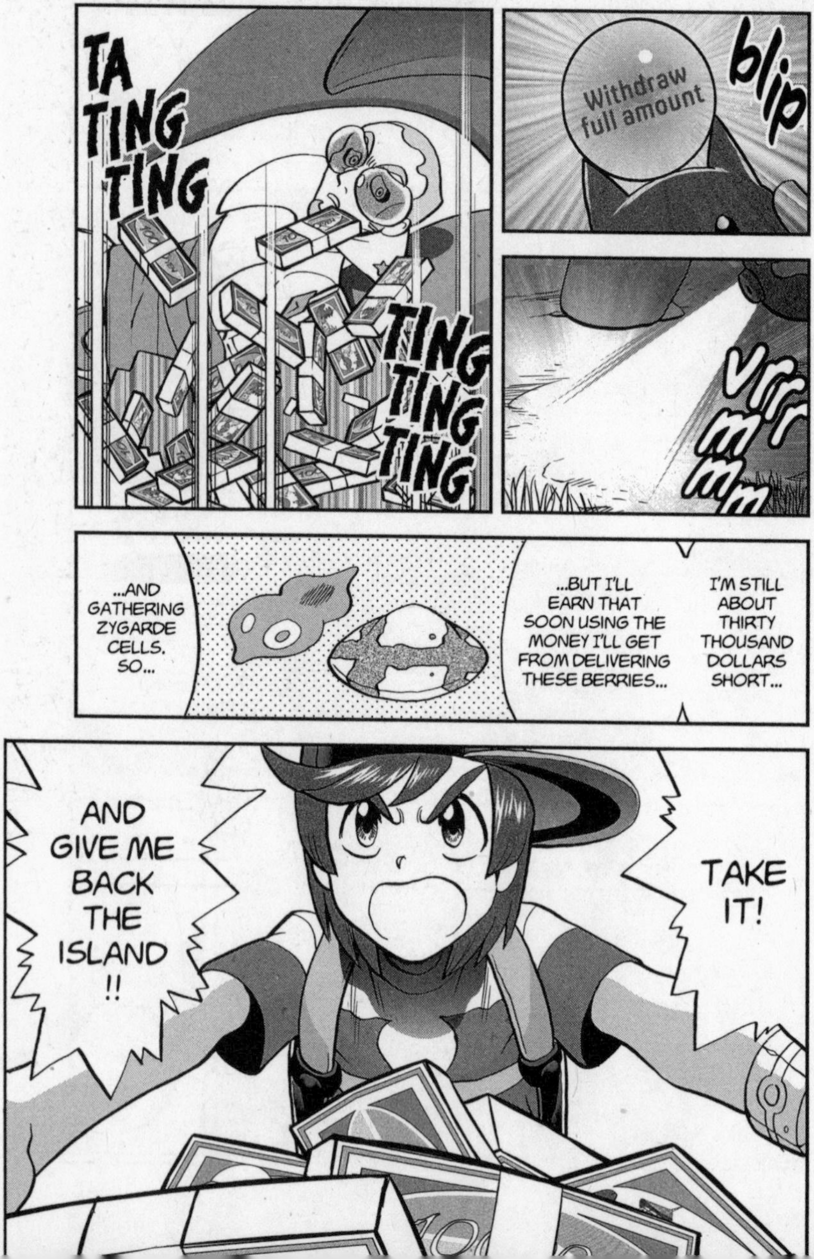
Withdraw full amount
blip
vrrrmmmmm
TA TING TING
TING TING TING TING
I'M STILL ABOUT THIRTY THOUSAND DOLLARS SHORT...
...BUT I'LL EARN THAT SOON USING THE MONEY I'LL GET FROM DELIVERING THESE BERRIES...
...AND GATHERING ZYGARDE CELLS. SO...
TAKE IT!
AND GIVE ME BACK THE ISLAND !!

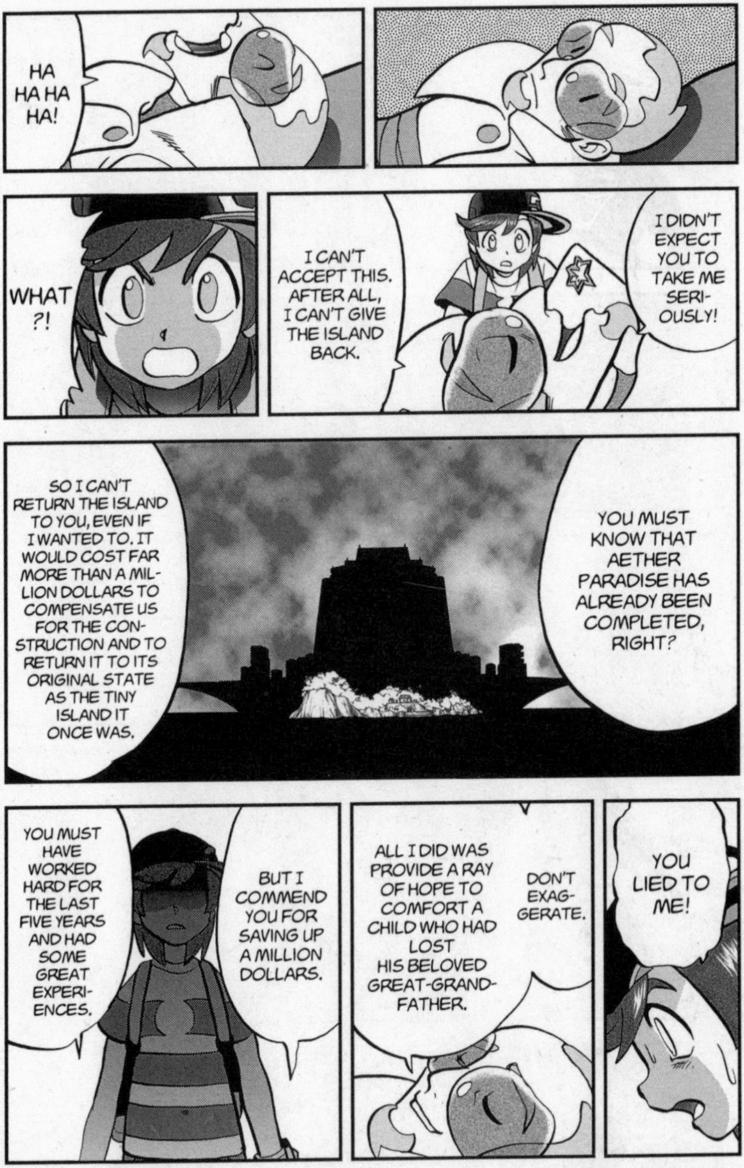
HA HA HA HA!
I DIDN'T EXPECT YOU TO TAKE ME SERI-OUSLY!
I CAN'T ACCEPT THIS. AFTER ALL, I CAN'T GIVE THE ISLAND BACK.
WHAT?!
YOU MUST KNOW THAT AETHER PARADISE HAS ALREADY BEEN COMPLETED, RIGHT?
SO I CAN'T RETURN THE ISLAND TO YOU, EVEN IF I WANTED TO. IT WOULD COST FAR MORE THAN A MIL-LION DOLLARS TO COMPENSATE US FOR THE CON-STRUCTION AND TO RETURN IT TO ITS ORIGINAL STATE AS THE TINY ISLAND IT ONCE WAS.
YOU LIED TO ME!
DON'T EXAG-GERATE.
ALL I DID WAS PROVIDE A RAY OF HOPE TO COMFORT A CHILD WHO HAD LOST HIS BELOVED GREAT-GRAND-FATHER.
BUT I COMMEND YOU FOR SAVING UP A MILLION DOLLARS.
YOU MUST HAVE WORKED HARD FOR THE LAST FIVE YEARS AND HAD SOME GREAT EXPERI-ENCES.

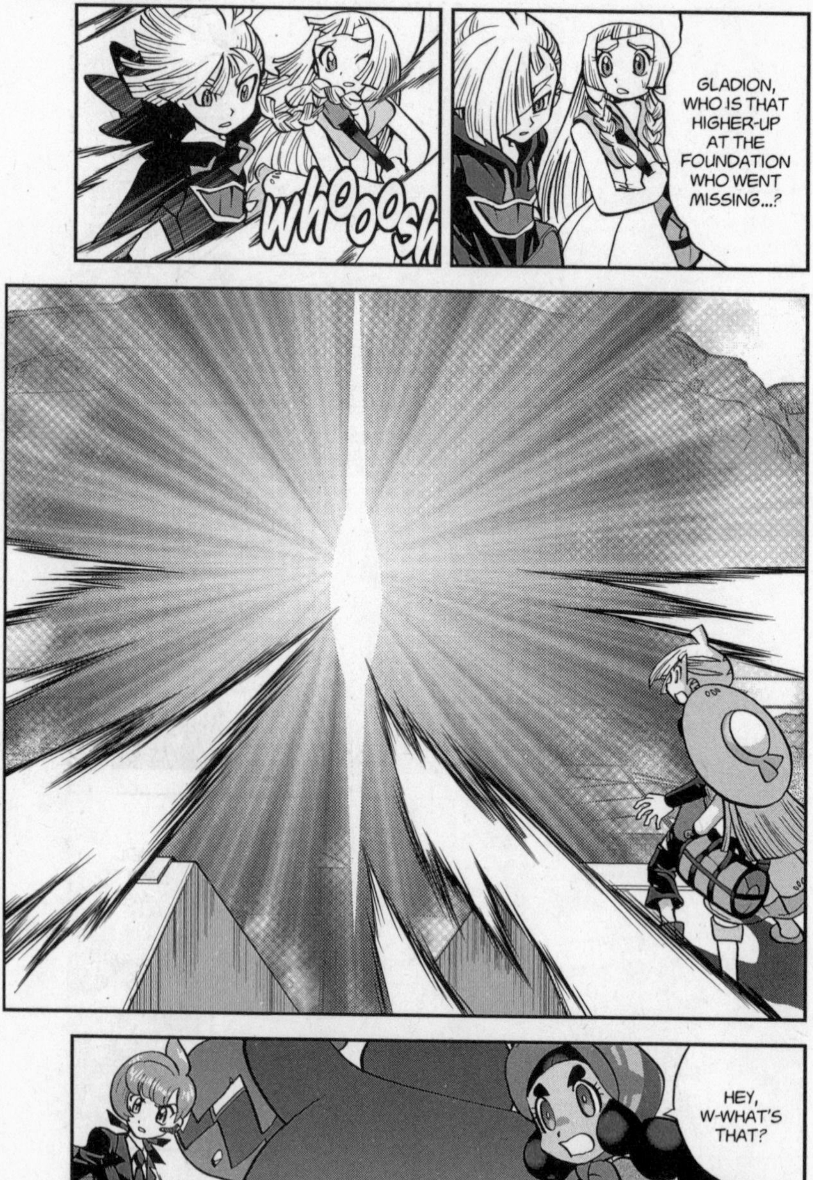
GLADION, WHO IS THAT HIGHER-UP AT THE FOUNDATION WHO WENT MISSING...?
whoooosh
HEY, W-WHAT'S THAT?

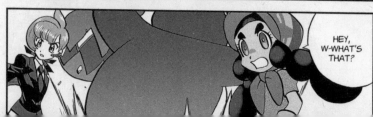

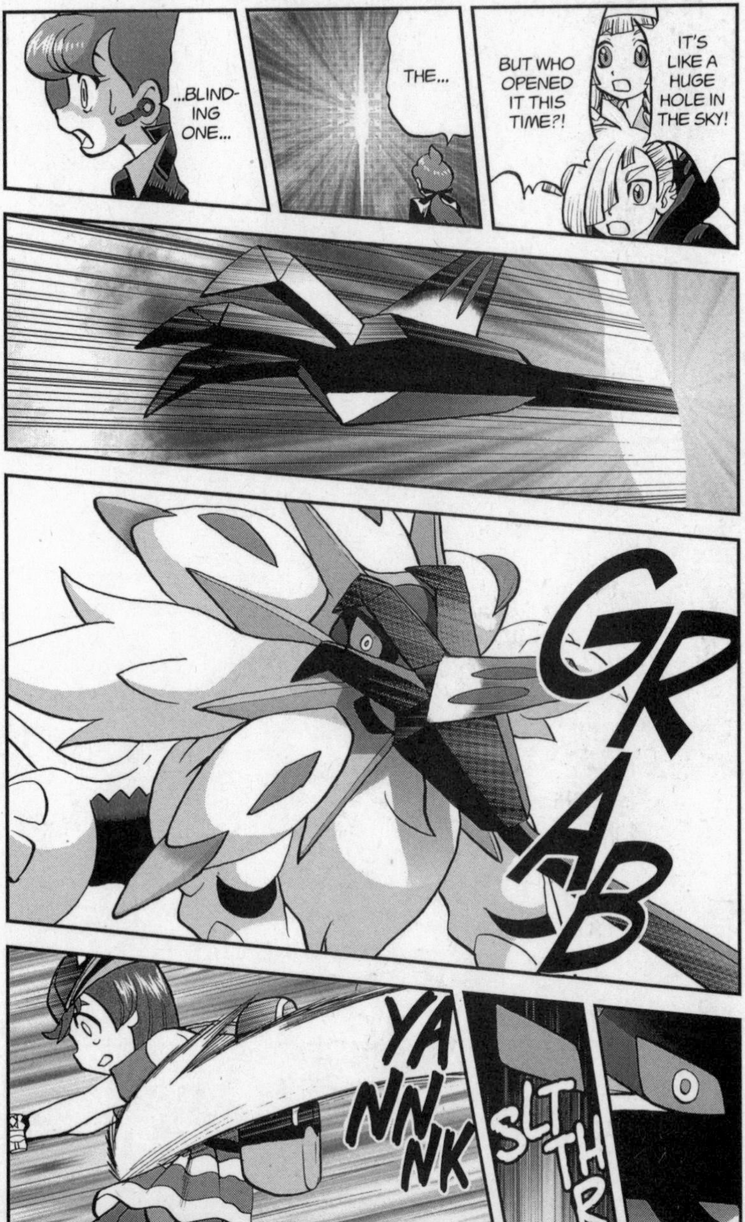
IT'S LIKE A HUGE HOLE IN THE SKY!
BUT WHO OPENED IT THIS TIME?!
THE...
...BLIND-ING ONE...
GRAB
SLTHR
YANNNNK

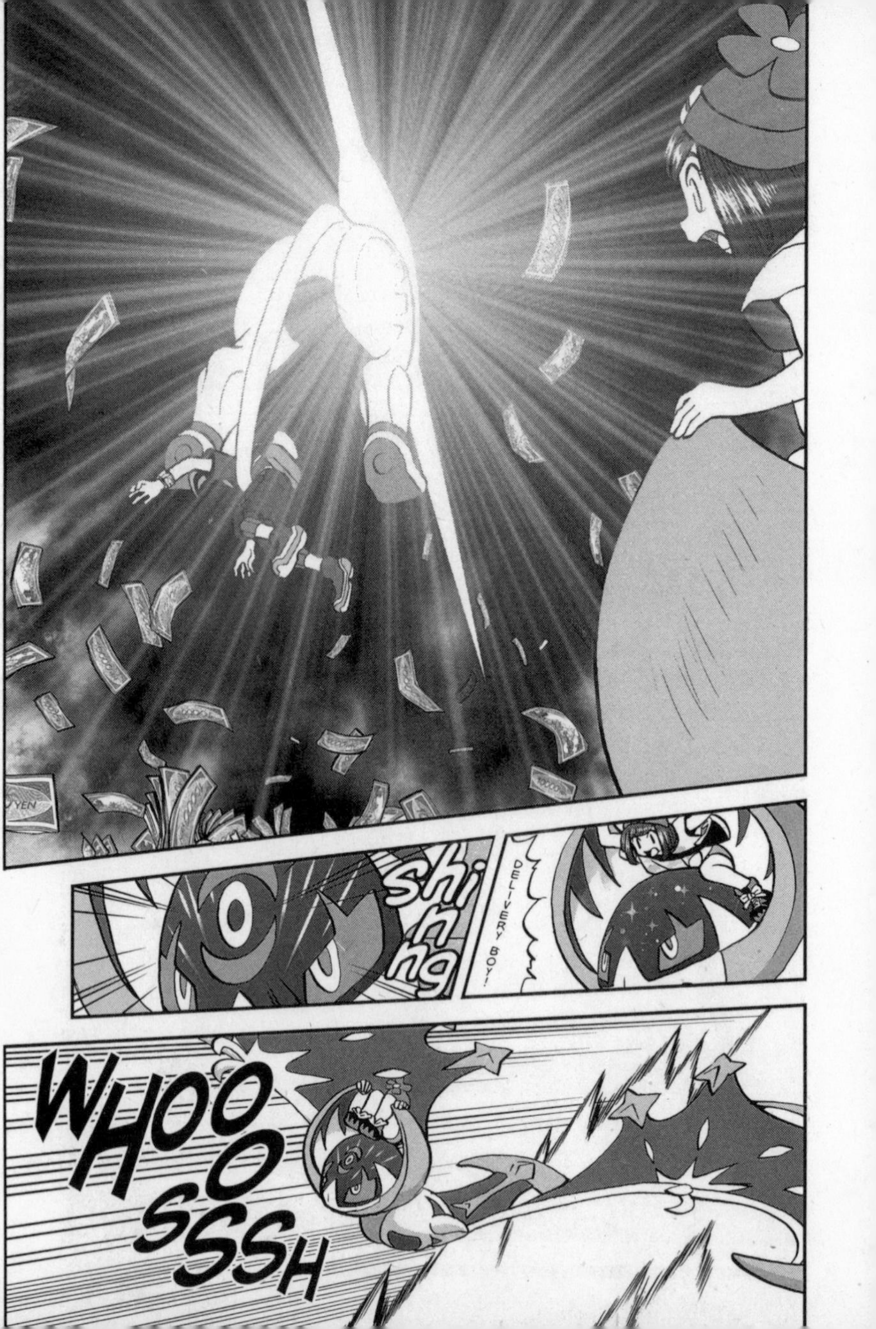
DELIVERY BOY!
shihhng
WHOOOOSSSSH

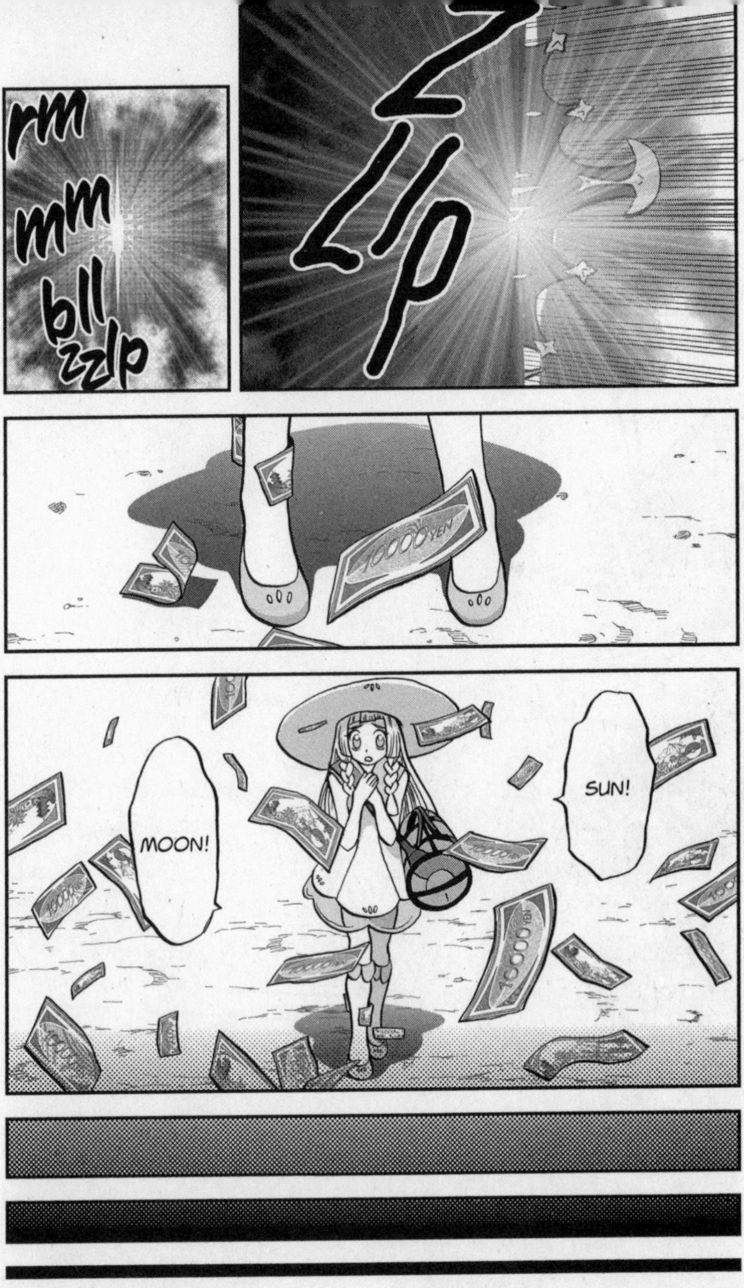
Zip
rmmmmbllzzlp
SUN!
MOON!

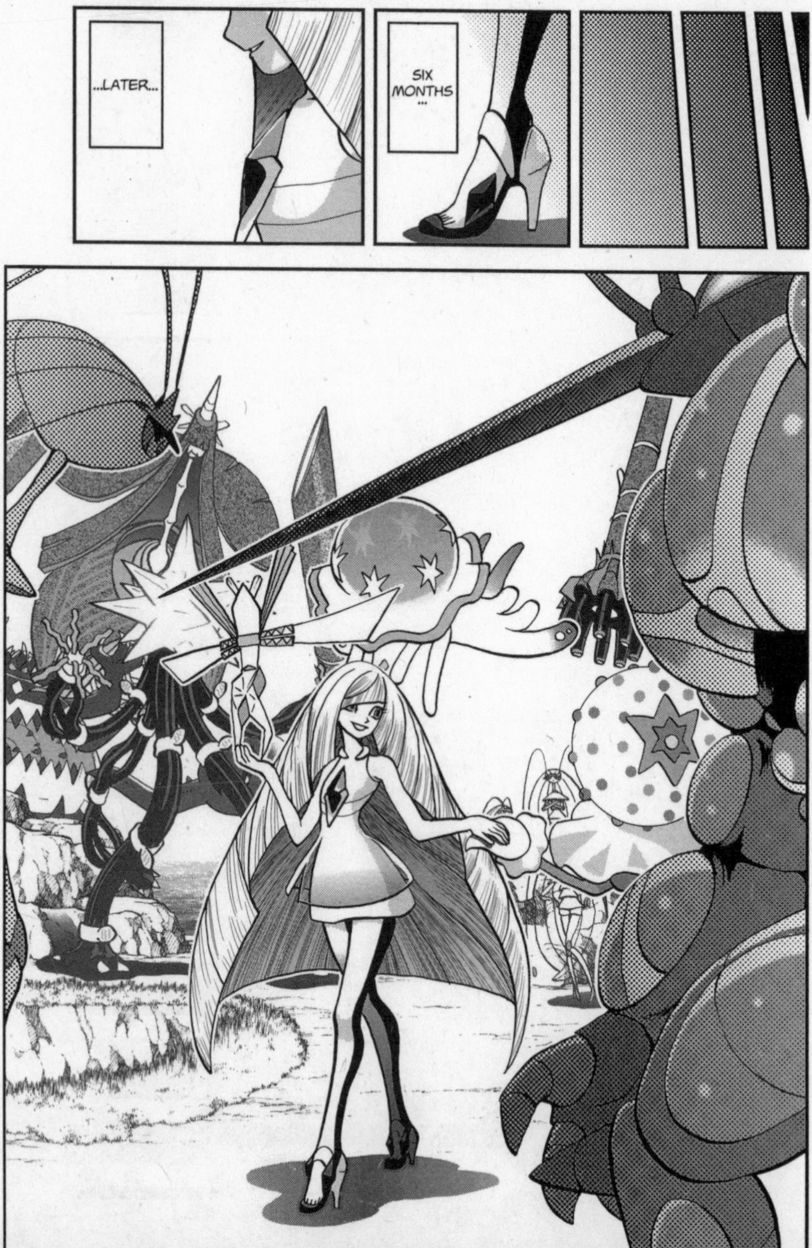
SIX MONTHS ...
...LATER...

Delivery Slip
SENDING ADDRESS
NAME
Time of Delivery:
ITEMS
8:00–10:00
10:00–12:00
12:00–14:00
14:00–16:00
16:00–18:00
18:00–20:00
Breakable
Perishable
Fragile
Hazardous
TO BE CONTINUED...

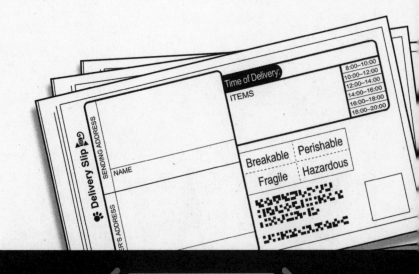

POKÉMON™

SUN & MOON

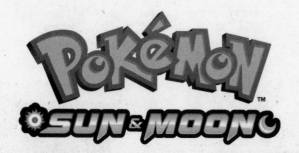

International Police Top Secret Files

Special topic!

Get to know the Ultra Beasts!

The Alola region is threatened by mysterious creatures from another world. What are they like? What follows is a report containing everything we know about them thus far.

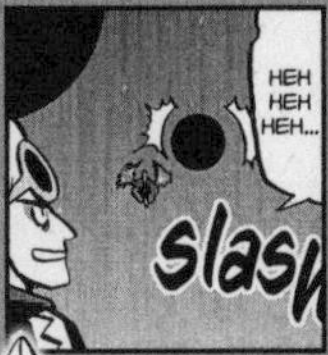

HEH HEH HEH...

▶ This hole, or rift, in the sky is a portal between the world of the Ultra Beasts and our world.

Nihilego

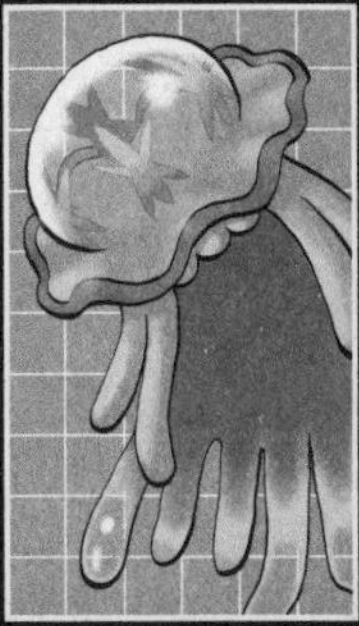

UB-01 (Symbiont)

A soft-bodied Ultra Beast who appeared in the battle at Ula'ula. It contains neurotoxins and is said to be a parasitic organism.

Discovered at:
Shady House

◆ Data ◆

Height: 3'11"
Weight: 122.4 lbs
Type: Rock, Poison
Ability: Beast Boost

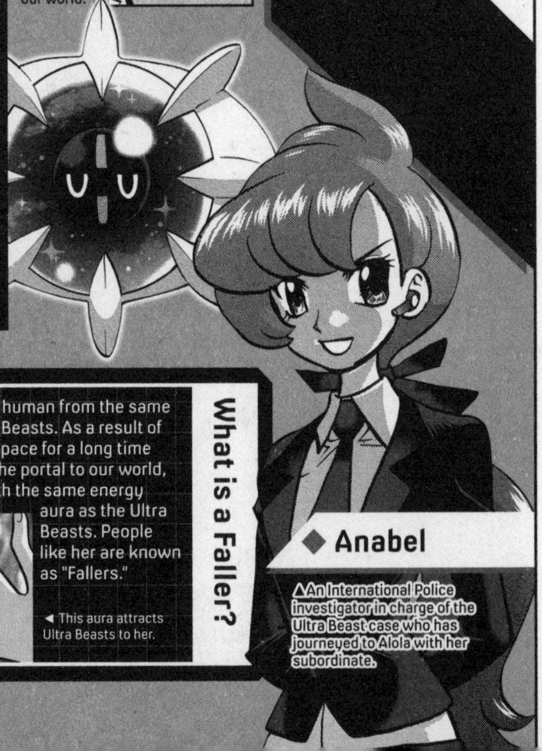

◆ Anabel

▲An International Police investigator in charge of the Ultra Beast case who has journeyed to Alola with her subordinate.

What is a Faller?

Anabel claims to be a human from the same dimension as the Ultra Beasts. As a result of drifting through Ultra Space for a long time before falling through the portal to our world, her body is cloaked with the same energy aura as the Ultra Beasts. People like her are known as "Fallers."

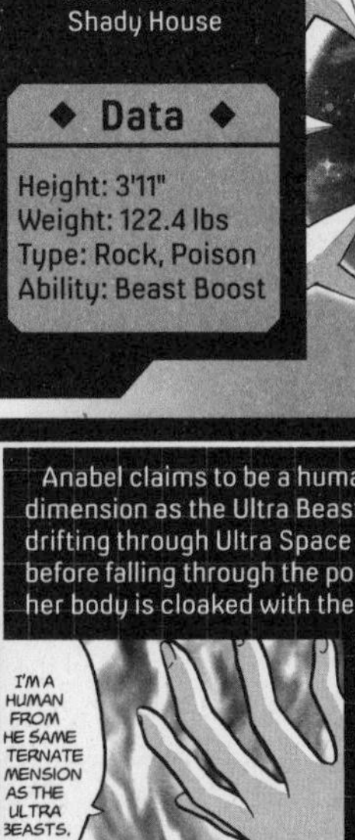

I'M A HUMAN FROM HE SAME TERNATE MENSION AS THE ULTRA 3EASTS.

◀ This aura attracts Ultra Beasts to her.

Xurkitree

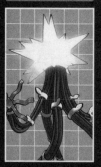

UB-03 (Lightning)

An Electric-type Ultra Beast who wields powerful electricity. It was strong enough to ward off a Tapu... How can it be defeated?!

Discovered at:
Lush Jungle

◆ Data ◆

Height: 12'06"
Weight: 220.5 lbs
Type: Electric
Ability: Beast Boost

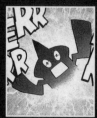

▲ Rotom Pokédex mustered up all its courage to face this Ultra Beast, yet was defeated in one blow.

Guzzlord

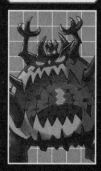

UB-05 (Glutton)

Its huge open mouth is an unforgettable sight. This Ultra Beast is said to be a big eater who swallows up everything within reach.

Discovered at:
Shady House

◆ Data ◆

Height: 18'01"
Weight: 1957.7 lbs
Type: Dark, Dragon
Ability: Beast Boost

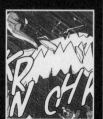

▲ These fangs are said to be capable of chewing through mountains. One chomp from these jaws and it's all over!

Celesteela

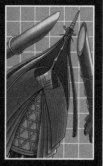

UB-04 (Blaster)

A massive Ultra Beast who attacks with its two bamboo-like arms. To our surprise, it can even fly.

Discovered at:
Shady House

◆ Data ◆

Height: 30'02"
Weight: 2204.4 lbs
Type: Steel, Flying
Ability: Beast Boost

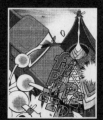

▲ Its steel body is extremely tough and seemingly capable of repelling any attack.

Blacephalon

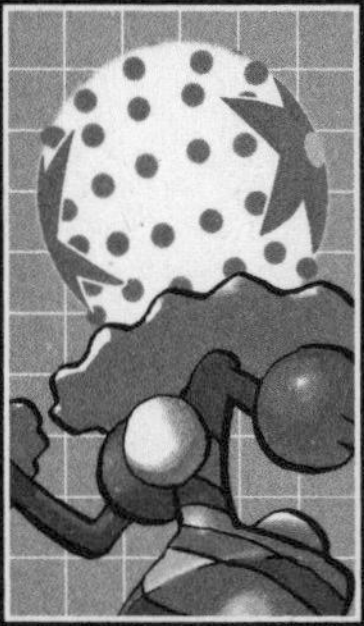

UB (Burst)

Its flashy, fiery body is beautiful to look at. As of this writing, we know of no strategies to counter its explosive attacks. It is a very powerful foe.

Discovered at:
Po Town

◆ Data ◆

Height: 5'11"
Weight: 28.7 lbs
Type: Fire, Ghost
Ability: Beast Boost

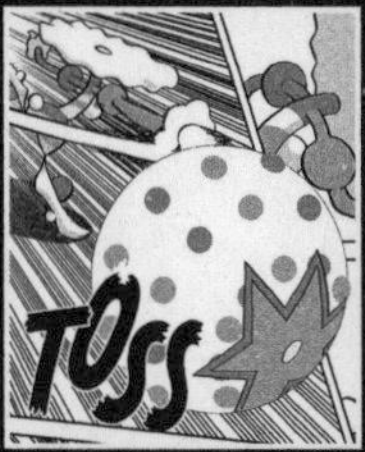
TOSS

▲ It is said to frighten people and then absorb their life force. Is this true?

Kartana

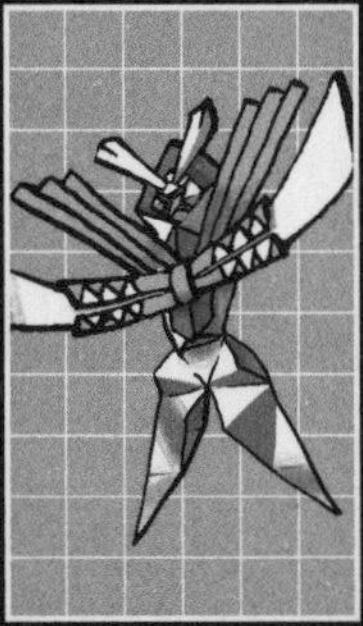

UB-04 (Blade)

Its most notable feature is its paper-thin body. Its limbs are very sharp and said to be capable of instantly slicing through metal. It might be possible to defeat it if you could attack it without physical contact.

Discovered at:
Melemele Meadow

◆ Data ◆

Height: 1'00"
Weight: 0.2 lbs
Type: Grass, Steel
Ability: Beast Boost

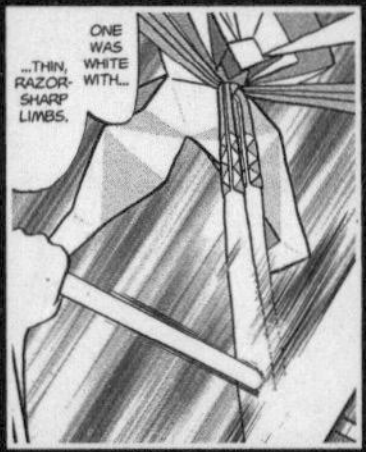
ONE WAS WHITE WITH...
...THIN, RAZOR-SHARP LIMBS.

▲ It sliced through this solid metal golf club. Its entire body is a blade.

Buzzwole

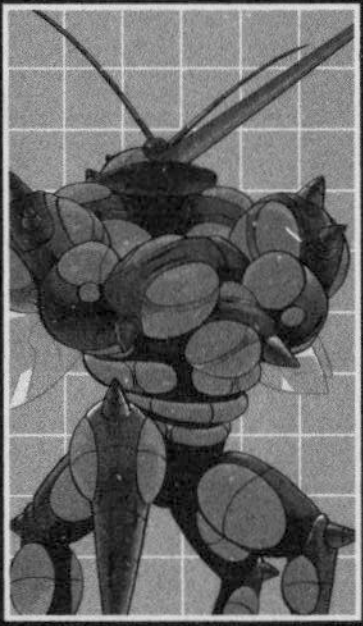

UB-02 (Absorption)

An Ultra Beast with rippling muscles. It moves like a posing body builder. Does its sharp mouth have a specialized function?

Discovered at:
Melemele Meadow

◆ Data ◆

Height: 7'10"
Weight: 735.5 lbs
Type: Bug, Fighting
Ability: Beast Boost

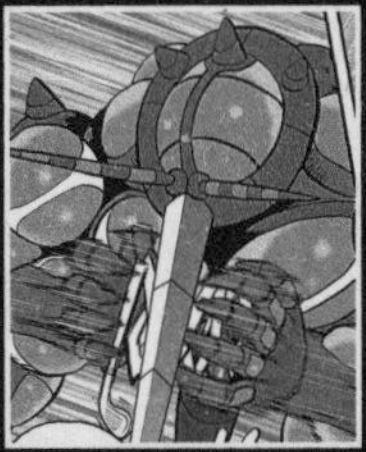

▲ It launched a surprise attack on Kahili when she had just returned to Alola.

Additional Investigation 1

Are Ultra Beasts Poké-mon?

We have noted that they have types, abilities and type advantages and disadvantages, so perhaps they are related to Pokémon in some way?

IS IT A POKÉMON, ROTOM?!
I DON'T HAVE ANY DATA ON IT YET, ZZT.

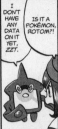

▶ Maybe as our research progresses we'll be able to add them to the Pokédex?

Additional Investigation 2

A Poké Ball that catches Ultra Beasts?

The International Police are currently investigating a way to create a Poké Ball that specializes in Ultra Beast captures. Who would be capable of creating a device like this?

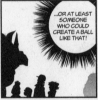

...OR AT LEAST SOMEONE WHO COULD CREATE A BALL LIKE THAT!

▲They have a hunch that this someone might be from the Alola region...

Additional Investigation 3

Are the emissaries of the moon and sun Ultra Beasts as well?

Solgaleo and Lunala evolved at the altar. When they were Cosmog, they enabled the Ultra Beasts to come to our dimension, so we believe they are connected in some way.

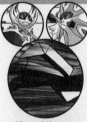

▲ Of especial interest is this black claw that appeared out of the blue...

Additional Investigation 4

Are there more Ultra Beasts?

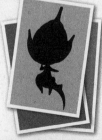

I found intel in the International Police data headquarters about an Ultra Beast unlike the eight we introduced today. What are its characteristics...?

▶ I sense trouble ahead. What will happen next in the Alola region...?!

Pheromosa

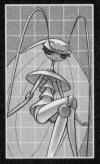

UB-02 (Beauty)

Its narrow, flexible body enables it to move quickly. However, that doesn't mean it's weak. It's actually very powerful as well as swift.

Discovered at:
Shady House

◆ Data ◆

Height: 5'11"
Weight: 55.1 lbs
Type: Bug, Fighting
Ability: Beast Boost

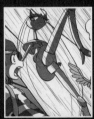

▲ It loves beautiful things and hates dirt.

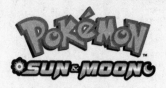

Pokémon Sun & Moon
Volume 8
VIZ Media Edition

Story by HIDENORI KUSAKA
Art by SATOSHI YAMAMOTO

©2020 The Pokémon Company International.
©1995–2019 Nintendo / Creatures Inc. / GAME FREAK inc.
TM, ®, and character names are trademarks of Nintendo.
POCKET MONSTERS SPECIAL SUN • MOON Vol. 4
by Hidenori KUSAKA, Satoshi YAMAMOTO
© 2017 Hidenori KUSAKA, Satoshi YAMAMOTO
All rights reserved.
Original Japanese edition published by SHOGAKUKAN.
English translation rights in the United States of America, Canada, the United Kingdom,
Ireland, Australia and New Zealand arranged with SHOGAKUKAN.

Original Cover Design—Hiroyuki KAWASOME (grafio)

English Adaptation—Bryant Turnage
Translation—Tetsuichiro Miyaki
Touch-Up & Lettering—Susan Daigle-Leach
Design—Alice Lewis
Editor—Annette Roman

Printed in the U.S.A.

Published by
VIZ Media, LLC
P.O. Box 77010
San Francisco, CA 94107

10 9 8 7 6 5 4 3 2 1
First printing, September 2020

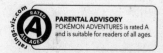
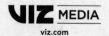

Coming Next Volume

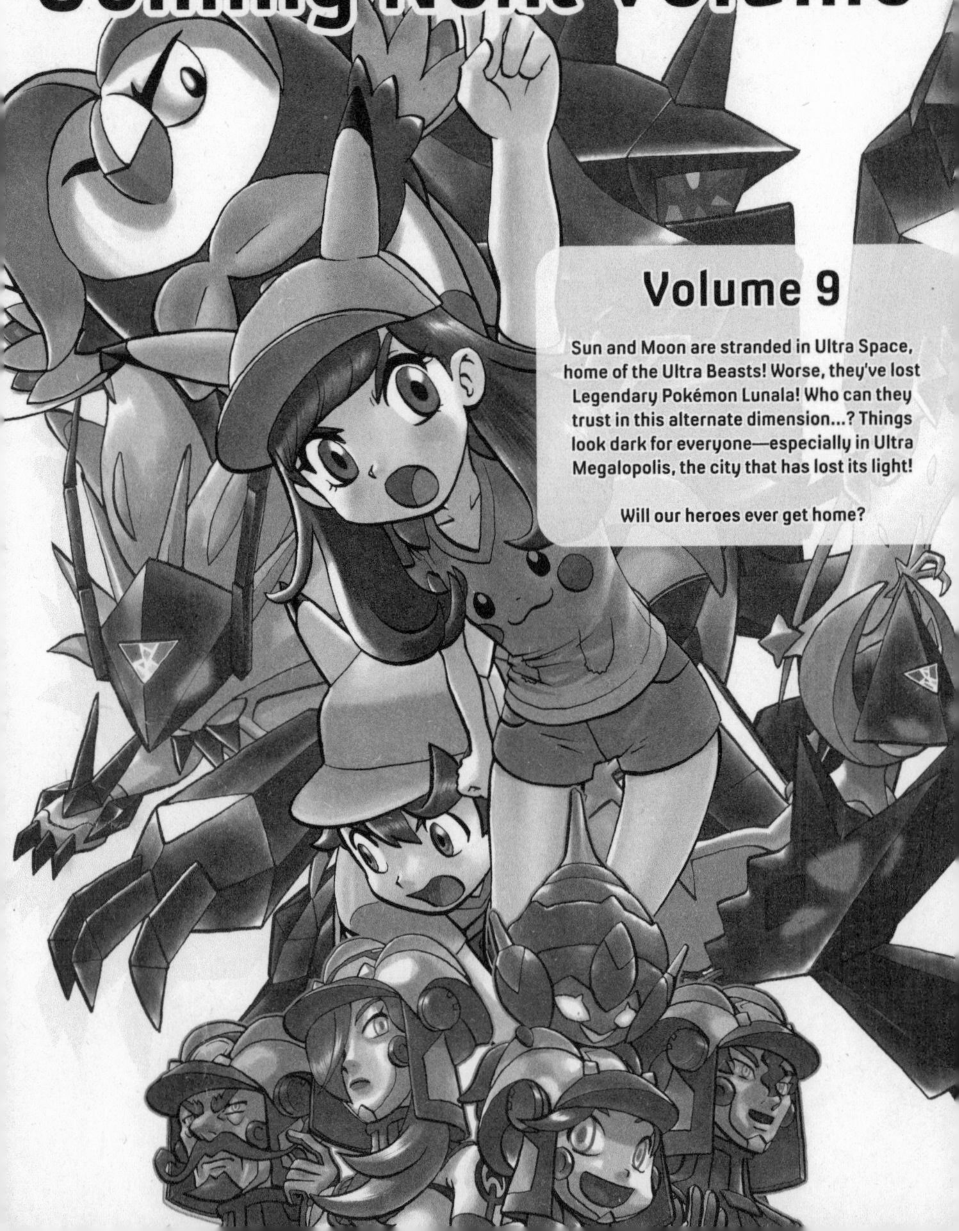

Volume 9

Sun and Moon are stranded in Ultra Space, home of the Ultra Beasts! Worse, they've lost Legendary Pokémon Lunala! Who can they trust in this alternate dimension...? Things look dark for everyone—especially in Ultra Megalopolis, the city that has lost its light!

Will our heroes ever get home?

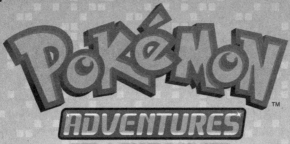
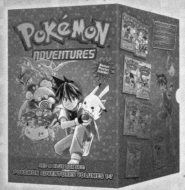
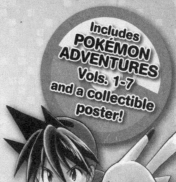

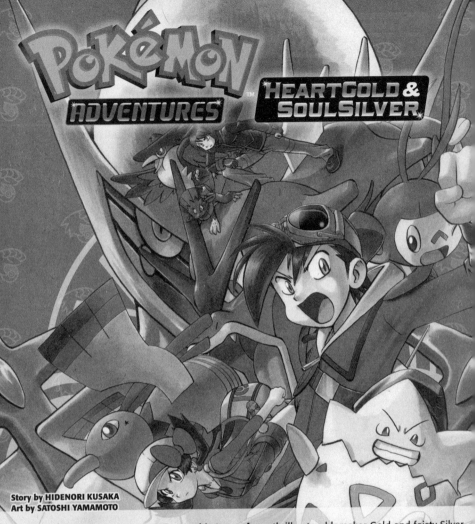
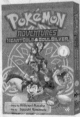 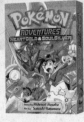

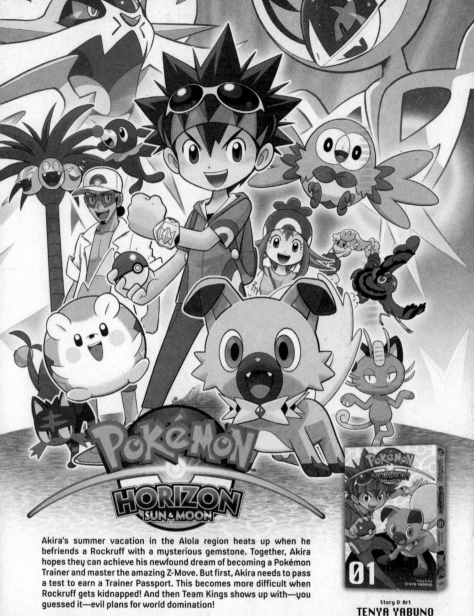

Pokémon
HORIZON
SUN & MOON

Akira's summer vacation in the Alola region heats up when he befriends a Rockruff with a mysterious gemstone. Together, Akira hopes they can achieve his newfound dream of becoming a Pokémon Trainer and master the amazing Z-Move. But first, Akira needs to pass a test to earn a Trainer Passport. This becomes more difficult when Rockruff gets kidnapped! And then Team Kings shows up with—you guessed it—evil plans for world domination!

Story & Art
TENYA YABUNO

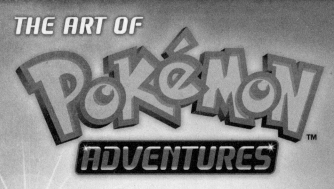

POKÉMON ADVENTURES 20TH ANNIVERSARY ILLUSTRATION BOOK

THE ART OF POKÉMON™ ADVENTURES

THE ART OF
POKÉMON
ADVENTURES
SATOSHI YAMAMOTO

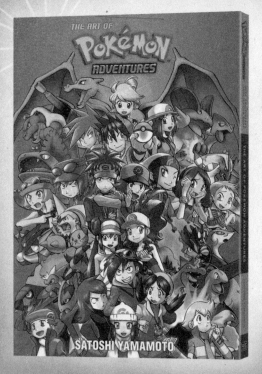

STORY AND ART BY
Satoshi Yamamoto

A collection of beautiful full-color art from the artist of the Pokémon Adventures graphic novel series! In addition to illustrations of your favorite Pokémon, this vibrant volume includes exclusive sketches and storyboards, four pull-out posters, and an exclusive manga side story!

VIZ

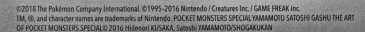

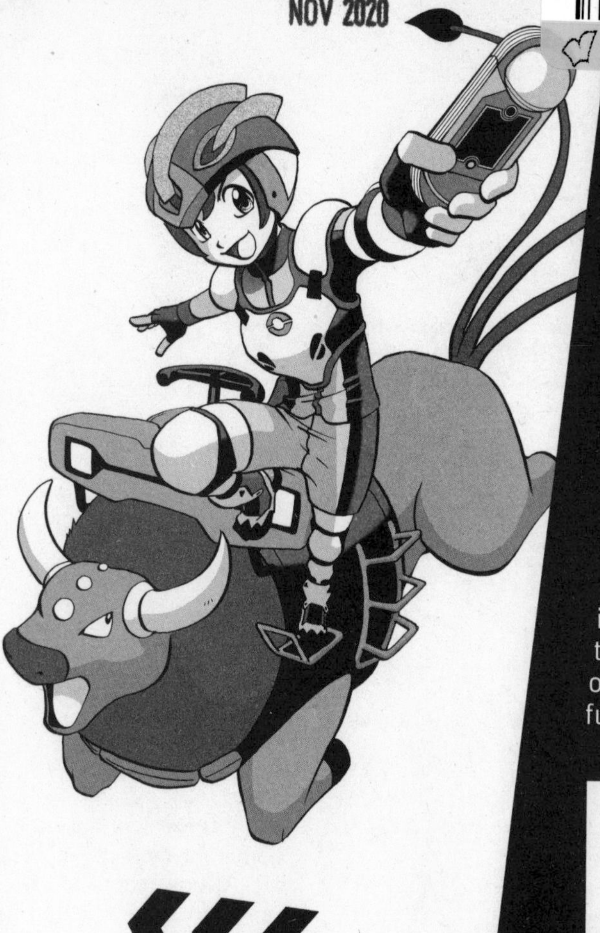

THIS IS THE END OF THIS GRAPHIC NOVEL!

To properly enjoy this VIZ Media graphic novel, please turn it around and begin reading from right to left.

This book has been printed in the original Japanese format in order to preserve the orientation of the original artwork. Have fun with it!

READ THIS WAY!

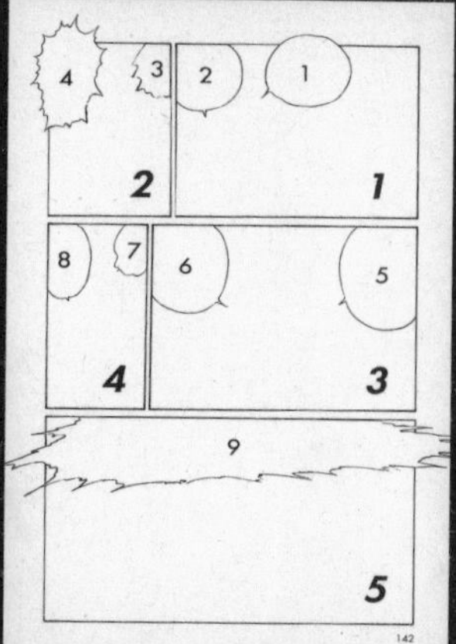
1
2
3
4
5
6
7
8
9

Follow the action this way.